SIGHT AND SINNERS

A Men of London Romance

Susan Mac Nicol

THE MEN OF LONDON

From Charing Cross to Waterloo, there's no escaping love.

SEEING THROUGH…

28-year-old Draven Samuels has a tragic past, but as an investigator with a high-profile London company he now gets what he wants. Tough, sarcastic, and sceptical, he has no patience for lies and even less for people who waste his time. Even if they're as beautiful as the wild and dark-haired Taylor Abelard. Especially when they're talking over the body of a murder victim.

THE DARKNESS

Psychic Taylor Abelard is used to people calling him a freak. He can see past events and feel the ghostly vibrations of people close to him who've passed on. It's why he doesn't get too close to the living. But this time, against his better judgment, despite Draven's mocking rejoinders, Taylor will get closer than ever before. The mystery of a dead friend will lead the two men down a dark and seedy trail of blackmail and lies. Add in the heartbreak of a family tragedy, and events lead them straight into each other's arms. By the end of this night, all their demons will have risen—and been banished with the dawn.

SIGHT AND SINNERS

A Men of London romance

Susan Mac Nicol

www.BOROUGHSPUBLISHINGGROUP.com

SIGHT AND SINNERS
Copyright © 2015 Susan Elaine Mac Nicol

ISBN 978-1942886-27-3

For all those staff who take care of people in critical care and intensive care wards. They do a tireless job looking after patients who sometimes aren't able to tell them how they feel, like Jude, and I think that must be terribly frustrating and heart-wrenching. I've had two family members in this situation, and I can tell you it sucks: for the patient, for the family, and for the nursing staff who sometimes have to simply make those people as comfortable as they can. For all of you who take care of the people we love when we can't—I thank you from the bottom of my heart.

6

CONTENTS

SIGHT AND SINNERS

Chapter 1

The man Taylor was blowing definitely didn't know how the hell to keep quiet. Taylor's lips were wrapped around his dick, while above him a man stood, panting and moaning, turning the air blue with his curses. Taylor stopped what he was doing, making the blow-job recipient groan in dismay, and glared at the sweaty face above him.

"For Christ's sake, Georgie, can you stop it with the fucking porn noises?" He glanced around him nervously. "This is where I work, damn it, and if anyone hears you they'll come outside to see what all the fuss is about."

Georgie's wide eyes cast a quick glance around the deserted alleyway behind 'Music Mayhem' where Taylor was employed, then looked down at Taylor kneeling between his legs.

"Sorry, mate, it's just that you're so damn good at this and it's been a while."

Taylor felt a surge of pride at that praise and went back to what he'd been doing. A few minutes later, he'd successfully made Georgie blow his load, while keeping the ruckus to a few grunts and sighs, and Taylor himself had been jacked off by Georgie's rough hands. He watched as the satisfied thirty-year-old bricklayer went back to the building site he worked at. Taylor rubbed his mouth, still tasting *eau de* hunky builder and sighed. He and Georgie were a long-standing arrangement, buddies even to the point of sharing a few beers after work, but Taylor was really getting fed up of the casual sexual encounters. He wanted something else. A Gideon and Eddie relationship, perhaps.

Oh yes, that would be an idea. I could stop all this damn nonsense in cold alleyways.

Taylor gave another deep sigh, made sure he had no stray spunk on his clothing and opened the back alley door to get back to work.

Sometimes life sucked.

*****

Blood and faeces. They were pungent smells that ripped into his nostrils and made his eyes water. The soft light of the dimly lit room cast shadows, gargoyles looming on red speckled walls. Somewhere in the room, a clock did what it was made to do. *Tick. Tick. Tick.* The air was heavy with the scent of death, redolent with grief and pain. It sucked the breath out of his body, leaving him helpless, useless.

Taylor screamed, gut-wrenching sounds that pierced through the heaviness of the air of his bedroom, as he fought his way out of the hell he found himself in. His hands grasped at bed covers that were already creased and wet with sweat and as his eyes snapped open in panic and despair. He took a deep, shuddering breath and shot upright in bed.

It was a chilly February night and although the window was open to let cool air in, the room was stuffy and smelled stale. Taylor thudded back against the wall and shivered as his naked back hit the peeling plaster, causing goose bumps to form on his clammy skin.

His bedroom door was flung open and a warm, male-scented bundle leapt onto his bed, wiry arms reaching for him to pull him close against a silky chest.

"Oh my God, Tay, you fucking scared me to death with that scream of yours!" Taylor's housemate, Leslie, gazed at him in horror from eyes still crusted in sleep and hollowed with dark shadows. The last few nights had been keeping Leslie awake as well, as he came to Taylor's aid when the nightmares hit with the force of an Acme sledgehammer raining down upon Taylor's head.

"What the hell is going on, sweetie? Where are these horrible dreams coming from?" Leslie's dark eyes framed with long lashes regarded Taylor with concern and fear. Taylor shuddered as Leslie's fingers combed themselves though his sticky, wet hair and the closeness of his slim body gave solace to Taylor's shaking form.

"The fuck I know, *chéri.*" Taylor heaved a deep breath. His French roots were buried deep and he didn't have a good grasp of the language apart from schoolboy-type phrases when he and his family had travelled to Provence for family holidays. His father had insisted on English at home despite his Mauritian-born mother speaking French. "It's the third time this week, different each time but still the same, you know?"

Leslie stared at him blankly. Taylor sighed and shifted in the bed, grimacing at the boxers stuck in the crack of his backside and groin. He reached down to pull them out and stop the constriction currently threatening to dissect his balls in half. Leslie let him go and sat back, his blue silk pyjama-clad body curling like a cat against the wall. Despite his emotional state, Taylor let out a soft chuckle. Even in the hot, humid nights, Leslie looked like a courtesan ready to please a prince. His innate sense of "good fashion or death" existed even when he slept. Leslie had always said if he died in his sleep, he wanted to go out with a sense of style.

"I mean, it's the same scene—the blood, the despair—but each time the dream shows me the whole thing from a different angle. It will stop soon, like it always does. It's just the whole initial phase thing of someone's death that affects me."

Not for the first time Taylor cursed his abilities, abilities that had plagued him since he was five years old. This whole "psychic" element of his psyche was really started to piss him off. He hadn't asked for it and he as sure as fuck didn't really want it.

But if I hadn't got this ability, I wouldn't have been able to help Eddie find Luke. Luke would have died.

Some months ago, using his abilities, Taylor had managed to help his ex-housemate, Eddie, prevent his younger cousin from dying from a suicide attempt.

"But you normally only feel this sort of thing if you're close to someone, Tay; that's how you say it works." Leslie's voice trembled. "So it must be someone you know, or somebody they are close to." His eyes widened. "Oh God, it can't be Eddie or Gideon, can it? Please tell me they're okay." He bounced on the bed in agitation, his dark black bangs falling over his face, obscuring cobalt blue eyes. "Could it be your dad?"

Taylor reached out and stayed his friend's anxious movements. "No, Leslie, it's none of them." Eddie had moved in a month ago with his boyfriend, Gideon, into the flat above the restaurant Gideon owned in Soho. "The lads are probably rutting like rabbits even as we speak."

Leslie gave a small giggle and Taylor smiled tiredly.

"As for my dad…" His face twisted. "I'm not that close to him anymore since mum died and he remarried. The last time I spoke to him was about two months ago." He shrugged. He'd intended going home to Bristol for Christmas but his father had told him he and Meg were going on a skiing holiday. So Taylor had spent the festive season with his friends instead.

He leaned back and reached over for his packet of cigarettes on the nightstand. He didn't miss Leslie's gimlet-eyed stare but he ignored it. He lit one up and took a deep, satisfying drag, making sure he didn't blow smoke anywhere near Leslie. He knew he'd get smacked if he did.

"You do know those things are going to kill you, right?" Leslie's voice was disapproving.

Taylor shrugged. "Something will one day. We never know when it's going to hit." Even to his own ears, his voice was bitter. Lately Taylor had been so taken over by his psychic abilities that his tiredness and the constant drain on his energies was beginning to defeat him. It was why he'd started smoking again after two years of abstinence. He had no idea why he was so in tune with the dead and the dying lately, but it seemed he was on high alert, that all the psychic karma in the fucking universe was raining down on his head.

Leslie's beautiful face darkened. "Stop it. I know you've had some really tough nights recently, but you need to suck it up. Something out there"—he waved a pale, long-fingered hand—"is going on with someone you know and that's why you're all tuning-forky."

Taylor took another drag of his cigarette and blew a lazy smoke ring in the air. It wafted toward Leslie. Taylor flapped it away in a panic.

"I have no idea who it can be though. Yes, I need to be pretty aware of someone before it affects me like this but everyone I know—small circle though that may be—is fit and healthy and I haven't got a clue who's in trouble."

He sucked the last bit of life out of his cigarette then stabbed it into the ashtray on the table. He leaned back against the wall and closed his eyes, his weariness soaking into his body.

Leslie regarded him thoughtfully. "How long has it been since you had any?"

Taylor opened one eye to look at his friend. "Are you talking anal sex, blow jobs, frotting, hand jobs, rimming …be more specific, Leslie." His tone was amused.

Leslie bounced on the bed, his eyes wide and his hands flapping in true Leslie style. "I mean, if you'd had a one-night stand, or a back-alley quickie…" He pursed his lips in that adorable pouty way he had and Taylor was entranced at the sight. "And I mean a back alley behind a building, not your back alley…although that works as well. Maybe it might be one of those guys you're feeling?"

Taylor had to admit the thought had crossed his mind. What he hadn't wanted to admit was that a casual encounter could affect him this way, as that would mean his abilities were more vulnerable now. He needed significant emotional closeness to pick up on the vibrations and emotions of a person, or something or someone affecting that person. But if what Leslie was suggesting was true, it meant that last night's frantic blow job behind the music store with Georgie, the quick, messy sex last week in the toilet stall of a club down the road, and the urgent mutual hand job in a car two weeks ago might all be related to what he now felt. And Taylor wasn't sure he could cope with that amount of mental and emotional stress.

He drew back the covers to his bed. "I'm too tired to think about it now. Come on, get in," he murmured. "I could do with someone beside me tonight." Not for the first time he wondered why he and Leslie had never taken their nightly cuddles and comforts any further. Sure, they'd shared a couple of hot kisses and jerked each other off once or twice, but neither of them had any inclination to pursue a real relationship. They were simply good friends. Leslie slid into the bed beside Taylor, the silk of his pyjamas a sensual touch against Taylor's bare back, his body warmth welcome. He pulled the covers over them as Leslie snuggled in behind him.

"Watch what you do with that thing," Taylor muttered. "I don't know where it's been."

Leslie chuckled softly. "And I'm not going to tell you," he retorted. "Suffice it to say lately it hasn't seen much action, so honestly? I can't promise I won't ravish you while you sleep."

"Well, slip it in quietly," Taylor said sleepily as his eyes shut. "And make sure you stick a sleeve on it before you do. I don't want to get pregnant."

Leslie's sweet laugh echoed in his ears as he fell asleep.

Chapter 2

Draven Samuels swore loudly and threw the mug he was holding across the room. It flew through the air like a cricket ball to a batsman and came to a stop when it hit the wall. Dark fluid spun out of it like an explosion of crap from a baby and the mug shattered into shards, which spiralled down to the floor. Draven watched the mayhem he'd caused as his hands clenched at his sides and his lips curled.

"Fucking stupid bastard," he growled. He paced around the room resembling a tawny cougar ready to spring. Lithe, taut and infinitely dangerous. He ran a hand through his hair and swore again.

"Fucker. I can't believe he did this to me." His gut churned with pangs of guilt at thinking about what might be the reason for his recall. But if it was what he thought, it honestly hadn't been a big deal in his eyes—certainly not enough to be kicked off this case.

He picked up the piece of paper currently residing innocently on the kitchen table and tore it in two with one vicious action. Then he did it again and let the pieces flutter to the floor. He kicked the pieces and then stomped on them for good measure. He'd printed the email purely so he could abuse it. When his temper tantrum was spent and he had his breathing under control, Draven whirled around to pick up his mobile. He jabbed numbers into the phone as if it was being punished then narrowed his eyes as he waited for the person on the other side to pick up.

"Clay Mortimer here." The drawled tones of the man on the other side only inflamed Draven more. He felt his face go puce and he looked at his phone as if were a mortal enemy before raising it to his ear again. He went onto the offensive in his usual Draven way.

"You traitorous sack of shit. How the fuck could you do this to me, you arsehole?"

"Ah, Draven." The voice sounded amused and Draven bit his bottom lip to keep from spitting at the phone in fury. "I thought I'd be hearing from you. Got my email, did you?"

"You took me off the damn case, Clay. You're recalling me to London and letting that simpering twat Jeremy Flaherty take over from me. This was my case, and I should be the one to finish it."

Draven glared out across the waters of the Adriatic, the crystal blue sea no panacea at the moment to his anger. The city of Dubrovnik had been his home now for nearly a month, and the case he was working on for Mortimer Investigations on the outskirts of London was almost over. It had been a difficult decision to leave his younger brother Jude behind in the hospital for any length of time but it wasn't as if he'd know Draven was gone anyway. Draven was on tenterhooks every time his phone rang, thinking it might be news about Jude's condition. For better or worse, he wasn't sure which news he dreaded the most.

That thought didn't make him feel better and the sinking, hollow feeling in his stomach hadn't dissipated. Draven had hoped his anger would feel more righteous than it was. He'd tried to rationalise it, but the truth was he had fucked up. Badly. And now he was paying the price.

"You have to let me finish this one, Clay. I am so close to getting the bastard who stole the blueprints; I just need another week. I can do this, I promise. The fact Ian is involved…"

Clay's cool voice interrupted his ramblings. "That would be Ian Ramsey, our informant? The man you've been sleeping with and who now threatens to compromise this whole case that we've been working on for over six months?"

Draven growled again. "I haven't been sleeping with him. I've been fucking him. There's a difference. We're just bed buddies." He tried once again to rationalise it. "And it was only three times. It's not like I'm going to ask the guy to marry me and bear my children, for Christ's sake."

"As entertaining as the idea of you in a suit swearing fidelity and allegiance to one man is, Draven, the fact remains that this man, this informant, is a delicate asset and not one I need compromised in any way. If the powers that be in government found out you two had a relationship, purely carnal or not, it would undermine this agency's credibility, and no one, I repeat, no one, fucks with the credibility of my agency." Clay's voice was hardened steel and even Draven baulked. "Am I making myself quite clear?"

Draven scowled and mouthed "Fuck you" at his phone.

And fuck you, Ian, you miserable, smarmy little git for being so damn fuckable.

The irony of that inner thought didn't escape Draven and he snarled quietly.

"Ahh, you're still there then? I recognise that rather nasty sound. There are return air tickets to London downstairs at the reception desk. You leave tomorrow. Jeremy will arrive tonight and you can debrief him." Clay's voice was dry. "And by debrief him, Draven, I mean update him on the case, not yank his pants down and stick your dick in him like you did with Ian. Although I have to say, I'm not sure Jeremy swings your way so it would be one helluva surprise to him if you did."

To add fuel to Draven's fury, Clay Mortimer snorted in amusement.

His temper rose again. "You are so fucking funny, you know that, Clay? Fine. I'll tell all to good old Jeremy when he gets here but he isn't going to get the job done like I would and you know it. I screwed up with Ian but that doesn't affect my ability to do my job."

There was silence on the other end of the phone and for a minute Draven thought he might be given a reprieve. Then he heard a deep sigh.

"Draven, you are one of my best operatives. You're tough, driven and highly motivated. But you have this self-destructive flaw to screw things up and think with your dick. Ian Ramsey is, as we speak, trying to get a better deal for himself by saying he was sexually harassed by the man who was supposed to be watching and helping him—that would be you, by the way—to get the information we need to prove that Kyle Enterprises is stealing government secrets." He coughed. "He has video footage of the two of you going at it like weasels. He said you seduced him into sex to keep him sweet and on our side."

Draven's jaw dropped and his hands grew clammy.

That fucking handsome, sexy little tosser. He stitched me over. How the fuck did I lose my focus like that? And, weasels? I obviously need to work on my technique.

But he knew. It had been Ian's charm, his sparkling blue eyes and oh-so kissable mouth, that tight arse and flat abs encased in denim and tight tank tops that had sent the blood rushing to Draven's groin and led him to bend Ian over the couch, the balcony and the private casino table at the swanky Christo Club.

"Furthermore, I've had to eat humble pie and grovel a bit and you know that never goes down well with me. I've managed to salvage the situation and made him some promises I'm going to have to keep, but you fucked this one up. He played you, Draven. Like a bloody harp."

Draven stared blindly out into the falling twilight of the early February evening. He felt cold and more than a little sick to his stomach at the colossal mess-up he'd made because of a piece of arse. He couldn't justify his lapse in judgement any longer.

"Draven, are you there?"

God, does he actually sound worried about me? Jude, it looks like Clay does have a heart after all.

Draven had been one of Clay's men for the past six years and he'd been a great support to Draven, especially after the tragedy—the car accident that had killed Draven's parents and left his little brother in a coma. His boss had picked up a drunken and almost senseless Draven from the bars and pavements with monotonous regularity. However, friendship and compassion notwithstanding, Clay had blood like ice water when it came to business, and now Draven had let him down. A true blue British cock-up, no less.

"Yes, I'm here," he said quietly. "I'll be back in London tomorrow and you can haul me over the coals again then."

Clay's voice softened. "Draven, you fucked up. It happens. That doesn't detract from the fact that you've had more successes than failures and you're the best man on my team. Come home and we can find you another assignment." There was a low chuckle. "Maybe I can find you a woman to work with; then I don't have to worry about that dick of yours getting into trouble." He sniggered and Draven growled softly. "Come by the office tomorrow afternoon before you go home. We can talk then. And say hello to Jude for me when you see him. Tell him his Uncle Clay is thinking about him." His voice was warm with concern and Draven blinked, his throat tight.

The line went dead. Draven laid his phone down on the kitchen table and went to the fridge. He took out a bottle of Stolichnaya vodka and fetched a glass from the cupboard. Then he made his way out to the balcony and sat down to gaze with unseeing eyes across the ocean.

May as well finish the bottle so I don't waste it now I'm going home.

The fact the bottle was half full had not escaped him. He only hoped that he'd be sober enough to fly home the next morning without puking his guts out into a paper bag.

Chapter 3

Taylor sipped his rum and Coke and sighed as he gazed around the restaurant. Galileo's was one of his favourite places to eat, mainly because the sous-chef was one of his two best friends here in London. Eddie Tripp had been a housemate until he'd moved out and moved in with his new boyfriend, the owner of Galileo's. Gideon Kent was an acquired taste: a rather growly, sarcastic individual with a rather tragic incident in his past. Yet in Eddie's hands the man was putty. Genuinely slippery and completely mouldable goo. Taylor appreciated Eddie's choice. Gideon was very tasty indeed if you looked past the scowling.

The restaurant was frenetic, testament to the great service and exceptional food. Taylor had come here to celebrate the end of the nightmares that had plagued him recently. They'd ceased about two days ago, and while he wasn't sleeping well, he *was* sleeping. He hadn't yet found out who had come to a grim end or how but he knew he would sooner or later.

He'd wanted Leslie to come with him but Leslie had apparently got a hot date. Taylor just hoped the guy had stamina, as Leslie had spent the day anticipating what he would do to him. His friend could be extremely creative.

Taylor watched as a man entered the venue and stared around fiercely. He was definitely worth looking at, he mused idly. Broad shoulders, blond hair, a rather curvy arse and a pair of strong legs currently encased in black chinos. He was shown to a table near the window and Taylor tried not to be too obvious as he watched the front of house manager attend to her customer's needs.

I'd like to attend to his needs. I'm sure he would make me very needy too. God, why don't gay guys wear a button or something so we know whether it's worth pursuing?

Taylor smirked and watched the sexy stranger pick up his menu. As he did, he lifted his eyes. They met Taylor's, and for a minute Taylor lost his breath. Mr. Mysterious had eyes as dark as grey slate, with straight brows and the longest, sexiest eyelashes Taylor had ever seen. The two men stared at each other for a moment, the other man's gaze challenging and open, his eyebrows raised quizzically until finally Taylor dropped his glance. He looked down quickly at his plate of spaghetti Alfredo as if he'd discovered the Holy Grail in it. For some reason, that confident, sexy stare had unnerved him like no other. He thought the man looked rather familiar, but recognition eluded him.

Taylor fiddled with his fork, twirling some pasta onto it and raising it to his mouth. As he did so, he couldn't help notice that Mr. Mysterious was still staring at him, his gaze hooded. Taylor shovelled the food into his mouth then licked sauce off his lips. Twice. The man watching him tensed slightly then looked away as a waitress approached his side with a drink.

What the hell? I feel like I know him. And he seemed a little rattled at my lip licking. At least that worked. Perhaps he does bat for my team.

That idea made him smirk. He risked another quick glance over at the man as he sipped his drink. Blond and hunky had now got his food and was eating it in quick, economical bites as if he expected it to run away and he needed to eat it before it did. There was nothing sloppy about it, just focused, structured movements of his knife and fork. He ate what looked like a rather large steak, putting in between full, pink lips. He didn't look Taylor's way again.

Taylor appraised him idly and ran his tongue wetly around the rim of the glass, just in case he looked up. He had it on good authority that the move was a guaranteed show starter when he did it. He heard a gentle cough to his left side and glanced over. Gideon Kent stood there, his handsome face amused and his hazel eyes glinting in the dimmed light of the wall sconces.

"Seen something you like, Taylor?" His deep voice echoed softly in the quiet of the alcove where Taylor sat. Gideon looked immaculate in his dark blue tailored business suit, coupled with a pale blue button-down that hugged his muscular chest. If Gideon wasn't spoken for, Taylor would definitely have made a play for him. As it was, he felt guilty for lusting after the man when he was in a relationship with his best friend.

He waved a hand airily. "I was admiring the view, yeah. Wondering if he played on my team and whether I should go over and buy him a drink."

Gideon snorted. "Good luck with that. He might be on our side but Draven Samuels is a difficult bugger. Comes in here regularly and always tips the staff very well. But he's not an easy man to get to know."

"Draven? Unusual name. I like it." Taylor stared over at the man on the far side who was sipping what looked like Coke. "Funny thing is, I think I've met him before but I just can't put my finger on where."

Gideon turned and ran a critical eye around his restaurant before turning his attention back to Taylor. "Well, make whatever play you like but I don't want to find you in the bathroom stalls together."

Taylor opened his mouth to deny that he did that and Gideon laughed. "Remember who sleeps in my bed, Taylor. Eddie loves post-fuck conversation and he's told me a few stories. Not that it's any of my business; I just don't want jizz messing up my clean bathrooms." His nostrils flared and a small smile softened his lips. He sniffed once, a look of pure satisfaction on his face.

"I like the aftershave. Maybe Draven would like it too."

A light went on in Taylor's brain. He remembered Gideon had lost his sense of smell and taste in a bad fire some months back. Recently he'd begun to be able to smell again and Eddie had been as excited as all hell about that fact. You'd have thought he discovered the cure for all the afflictions of the human condition.

Gideon laughed and motioned toward the empty plate as Taylor eyed him with narrowed eyes. "Looks like you enjoyed your food. I'll ask Eddie to send you out an Italian coffee, on the house. I know that's what you usually have to finish off a meal." He checked his watch. "Gotta go. I might be the boss but I can't be seen to be slacking off. Say hi to that crazy roommate of yours. I'll tell Eddie you say hi." He grinned fondly. "The man is causing havoc in the kitchen tonight. He's broken two plates already."

He waved and disappeared into the busy hive of the restaurant. Taylor hadn't even had time to thank him for the free drink. Sighing, he looked over at the mysterious Draven Samuels. He was absorbed in some sort of pudding, poking at it with a fierce scowl that looked as if he thought it might bite him. Taylor choked back a laugh. Well, at least he knew the man's name now. He grinned wickedly. He'd take the bull by the horns and go over there, buy the man a drink. Perhaps he could seal the deal on this one; he just had to make his move. Taylor licked the rim of his glass again and smiled.

*****

Draven prodded at his mocha latte ice cream dish and scowled. It wasn't the pudding, dribbled with some sort of delicious honey sauce and peppered with pecan nut chips that were causing his ire. No, it was a honey of another sort. It was the man across the room who'd licked his lips like some sort of porn star then ran his pink tongue around the rim of his glass. Draven wanted desperately to feel that tongue circling another kind of rim. But now he'd remembered where he'd seen the younger man before, and there was no fucking way on God's green earth that he was pursuing his initial instinct to take the man home and screw the lip-licking crap out of him.

When he'd first laid eyes on him, his dick had reared to attention like a meerkat popping out of its hole. The man had every attribute that pushed Draven's "want it, have to have it" buttons. A little younger than him, with light, coffee-coloured skin, thick, curly black hair down to his shoulders, what looked like a trim and wiry physique under a tight red polo shirt, well-muscled arms that led to fingers that could definitely strum what they liked, and lips beneath a hint of dark stubble—those damn lips again—that would look just as good sucking his cock as they did licking sauce off. He'd seen Gideon wander over to him and have a conversation and then watched as Brown Eyes went back to trying to be sexy. He was succeeding if the steel in Draven's chinos was anything to go by.

He attacked his dessert with gusto, lamenting each time he stabbed the spoon into the goo that was melting in his bowl that he wouldn't get to take the man home tonight.

"Has that pudding offended you in any way?" The enquiry was delivered in an amused, warm tone. Draven knew who it was before he looked up. He schooled his face to show the required expression of diffidence and disinterest. The man from the table with the beautiful lips stood before him, a slight smile on his face, but Draven noticed the hands fidgeting at his sides. Brown Eyes wasn't as confident as he made himself out to be.

"I'm sorry. Did you say something?" He stared at the younger man, trying to convey the fact he wasn't interested even when he knew it was a lie. He'd felt the same thing the first time they'd met as well.

Warm, dark caramel eyes stared into his appraisingly. "Well, the way you were stabbing it, I thought it might have disagreed with something you said. You don't strike me as the kind of man who'd take kindly to being argued with."

Draven set his spoon down and leaned back in his chair. The man's smile faltered a little but he held Draven's gaze.

"I don't think we know each other well enough for you to make that assumption," Draven said sharply. "Anyway, is there something I can do for you?" He stared at the other man.

"I was going to ask if you wanted a drink." The man held out a hand. "My name's Taylor, by the way. Taylor Abelard."

Draven nodded. "I know who you are. And no, thanks. I have a drink." He held up his empty glass and waggled it then set it down and picked up his spoon.

"We've met before? Where? I thought you looked familiar but I couldn't remember where from..." Taylor's voice trailed off as Draven deliberately went back to eating the last remnants of his ice cream. He ignored Taylor's sharp, indrawn breath as he was deliberately dismissed.

"Aren't you going to at least answer my question? I'm sorry if I offended you offering you a drink but..." Taylor's voice was husky with anger.

Draven ignored him and continued eating, yet still the man didn't get the hint and move away. Instead, one slim hand reached down and plucked the spoon from between his fingers. Draven looked up, startled, as Taylor smiled and held the spoon away.

"You're quite rude, aren't you?" Taylor said conversationally. "You could just have said no thanks, politely."

"No thanks. Now piss off." Draven growled and reached for his spoon.

Taylor shook his head, his face set. "Oh no, you're not getting this back until you tell me where we met and why you're being such an arsehole."

Draven looked around the restaurant. "I'll just get the waitress to bring me another." He knew he was being childish, but his frustration at not following through on his desire and his knowledge of what this man did to people was like acid in his stomach.

"Fucker." Taylor said quietly, and at that insult, Draven looked up, his fists clenching. No one called him names like that, especially not beautiful men with kissable lips and the look of a dark angel.

"Give me back my fucking spoon." He made a move to rise out of his seat and Taylor moved forward, his hips just below the level of Draven's mouth and he swallowed at the sight of that silky groin. Taylor was wearing a pair of drawstring pants made out of some sort of soft, black material. Draven wanted to pull the knotted cord at his waist with his teeth and watch them slide off slim hips to the floor. The outline of Taylor's crotch was visible beneath the fabric, tantalisingly close.

"Just tell me where you know me from and I'll leave," Taylor said curtly. Draven could see from the implacable set of his shoulders and the hardened eyes that he'd have no peace until he told Taylor what he wanted to know.

"We met at an investigation a year ago, when Bobby Meredith went missing. Remember him?" Draven said bitingly. "Little kid with strawberry-blond hair, six years old, who was found in pieces under an oak tree in a field in Sussex."

He watched as Taylor's café au lait skin paled and he thought Taylor might pass out from the sick look on his face.

"Bobby?" Taylor said haltingly, and Draven watched his Adam's apple bob in his throat as he swallowed. "Yes, I remember Bobby…" His voice tailed off and he paled even more. Draven felt a spurt of satisfaction at being able to shake the man's composure. "You were consulted on that case to help 'find' him."

Taylor's body was trembling and he had a haunted look in his eyes as Draven continued. "His parents were friends of your parents, if I remember, and they thought you could use your *powers* to help. You used to babysit the kid from what I recall." He spat the word "powers" out with the derision he felt. "I was helping a friend of mine in the force do a psych profile for the guy we thought took him, and that was when we met. There in the field over the remains of Bobby Meredith. You were looking at part of his left leg when you passed out, if I recall." He had no idea where his viciousness came from and he knew it was totally out of line but at those last words, Taylor gave a strangled cry and spiralled senseless to the floor.

*****

"Taylor? Honey, come on back, okay? It's Eddie. Come on, bud. Wake up."

Groggily Taylor opened his eyes to stare into a pair of bright green ones that regarded him with concern. Eddie's face was pale, and his freckles stood out like raindrops on a pavement.

"There's my lad," Eddie crooned as he brushed a hand through Taylor's hair, lifting sweat-drenched strands from his cheek. "I thought you were never going to wake up."

Taylor struggled to a sitting position as Eddie helped him up. "I passed out?" he said faintly. "God, I'm sorry, I didn't mean to make you worry—"

He was in Gideon's office, seated in the big armchair in the corner of the room. There was a ring of worried faces surrounding him: Eddie, peering at him anxiously, Gideon regarding him with a concerned frown and...Draven-fucking-Samuels. He stood there with a scowl on his face.

But there was something else too. Guilt.

Taylor's temper rose at the fact that this man had caused such a reaction in him with a few choice words. Little Bobby's case was one that still resonated with Taylor, and hearing Draven speak so disparagingly of a little boy who had suffered horribly had cut him to the core. The scenes of Bobby's death and the bond he'd had with the child when he'd been asked to help find him still gave him nightmares.

"You motherfucker," he swore quietly as he gazed gimlet-eyed at the blond man. "What the hell are you still doing here? I'd have thought you'd have cut and run as soon as I hit the deck. You should have. Because when I get up I'm going to punch you in the damn face."

Taylor's legs still felt weak, so as tough as his threat might have sounded, he wasn't yet ready to play it out. Eddie turned slowly to Draven and stared at him frostily. Taylor knew him to usually be an easy-going man, but when his red-headed temper flared, no one was safe.

"What the fuck did you do to him?" Eddie demanded as he moved closer to Draven. "Tay, you want me to smack him for you?"

Gideon snorted and laid a hand on his boyfriend's arm. "Love, no one's smacking the patrons of my restaurant," he said in amusement. "Although if I find out Draven needs a good whack, I'm sure we can come to some arrangement outside." His brown eyes stared at Draven thoughtfully. "What did you do to Taylor to make him fall down like that? He looked like a puppet with the strings cut. I saw him pole axe from across the restaurant."

Taylor stood up, wobbling a bit as Eddie steadied him. "It was something he said that brought back a memory I'd rather forget," he said quietly. The fight had disappeared from him and all he wanted to do was get home and curl up into a ball, preferably with a bottle of something, and try and forget the world for a bit. "I'll be all right, Gideon. "

For the first time Draven spoke. "I'm sorry. I didn't mean to make you faint. I shouldn't have said what I did."

"You bastard," Taylor spat bitterly. "You think you can remind me about one of the worst events of my life and not have it affect me? You remembered all too well what it did to me the last time we met."

He'd remembered who Draven was now. He'd met him at the scene when they'd found Bobby's body. Well, where *he'd* found Bobby's body and helped apprehend a child killer. He'd been called in to help the family trace their missing child, and he'd succeeded. It hadn't been made common knowledge that it was his abilities that had done that. The police force was still wary of telling the general public that a psychic was assisting them in their enquiries and had succeeded where they hadn't.

The area where Bobby had been dumped had been a wooded area deep in a forest, and when Taylor had spotted the boy's dismembered limb lying in a bush of something with red berries, he'd thrown up then promptly passed out. The psychic energy and painful emotion emanating from the scene had been tremendous. Draven had been standing near the limb, a look of horror and pain on his face as he gazed down at what had once been a vibrant little boy.

The events after that hadn't been much better. When he'd come to, Taylor had heard the sneering comment from Draven about people abusing others and leading them on to try and make themselves heroes, and good old-fashioned investigative police work won out every time rather than these "frauds" who played havoc with grieving people's emotions. He'd had no doubt the nasty comments were directed at him.

"And just to set the records straight—*I* was the one who found Bobby and helped them get the guy who did it. The police kept it quiet and let the public think it was them because, well, because they didn't want people to know a *fraud* had done what they couldn't so far." He spat the word out and watched Draven's face pale. "I'm sure they would have found Bobby eventually. My mate Rick is a damn good copper and he'd have succeeded. But knowing I do what I do—he decided it was worth the chance. And I was more than happy to stay out of the limelight."

Gideon and Eddie's faces were a mixture of horror and anger as they gazed at Draven. They knew first hand of Taylor's propensity to "see" things.

"He's genuine," Eddie burst out vehemently. "I can vouch for that. I've been on the receiving end of his so-called 'fraudish' abilities."

"I said I was sorry." Draven's voice was even. "I don't believe in all this hocus-pocus crap so it's difficult to believe. Back then I saw you as someone just feasting off the grief of a family desperate to know what had happened to their kid. I didn't know."

"Yes, well, maybe next time you shouldn't let your mouth run away with you." Taylor was drained. He turned to Gideon and Eddie. "I need to go home. I'm knackered. Thanks for looking out for me, guys." He clapped Eddie on the arm and moved toward the door.

Gideon stopped him. "I'll run you home. I don't want you passing out again." He raised a finger at Taylor's protest. "No buts. Let's get your gear together—it's at reception—and go. Babe, I'll see you later." He grinned as he stared at Eddie. "And please don't beat up Draven when I'm gone. He might have been an arsehole but he's a paying customer." He cast a quick glance over at Draven then leaned over and gave Eddie a deep, loving kiss. Despite his bad mood and tiredness, Taylor smiled. He never tired of watching these two together. They'd been seeing each other for over six months now, and while Taylor missed his old housemate, he knew that Eddie belonged here with Gideon.

He moved toward the door, intent on collecting his belongings and getting the hell out of there, when Draven reached out a hand and gripped his shirt-sleeve. Taylor glared at him.

"Take your damn hand off me. Aren't you scared you'll catch something?"

Draven growled but removed his hand. "I just wanted to say I hope you feel better. But hey." He waved a hand. "Feel free to leave."

"I intend to," Taylor growled back.

God this man makes me want to punch him.

He followed Gideon out the door.

*****

Draven stood, a little nonplussed at all the fuss he'd caused and shot a quick look at Eddie when the man gave an exasperated puff. His dark red hair was sticking up on his head like a parrot's crest, probably because he'd taken off the chef's cap he had tucked in the front of his rather mucky apron. He regarded Draven with a look of dislike in his green eyes.

"So, you make a habit of being a bitch then?" His eyebrows cocked and he folded his wiry arms across an equally wiry chest. Draven could see the attraction of the man. He was a feisty little bantam ready to do battle.

Draven held back a weary chuckle. Telling the man that *would* probably earn him a beatdown. "Taylor's lucky to have you on his side. I guess before the glove hits the ground and you challenge me to a duel, I should get going myself. I still need to settle the bill. Everything happened a bit fast and I didn't get the chance."

Eddie waved a hand. "You're damn right you'll settle up. You're lucky I'm not charging you a surcharge for all the fuss tonight."

Draven smirked. "I thought this was Gideon's place? Aren't you just the chef?" The careless words were out before he could pull them back and he took an instinctive step back as Eddie's face darkened and he moved toward him.

"You truly are a bastard, aren't you?" Eddie poked a long boned finger at Draven's chest. "Just a warning. Don't cause Taylor any more grief. He's been through enough lately, what with all the damn nightmares and stuff," he broke off and sniffed. "Not that you'd care anyway. Now I hear a bus or something with your name on it. Time to go."

Draven got the impression Eddie would have preferred him to be under the bus instead of in it. He was hustled out of the office then Eddie closed the door behind him.

"You know where the pay desk is. Have a nice rest of your night, arsehole." He turned and strode off toward the kitchen, leaving Draven to pick up the pieces of his night.

Later that night as he drank whisky from a grimy tumbler, Draven had the strangest feeling that he'd be seeing Taylor Abelard again. Where that certainty came from, he didn't know. When he got into bed that night, he jacked off to the thought of caramel eyes and warm lips and pale tanned skin that writhed against his in sweat and passion.

Christ, the damned man had certainly left a lasting impression.

Chapter 4

A week later, Taylor sat at the dining room table and stared at the newspaper with a feeling of disbelief. He'd just showered and come down to have a plate of granola before leaving for work.

How can they be having a service for Drew? I didn't even know *he was dead.*

Now, though, the nightmares and events of the past few weeks now made terrible sense.

He swallowed bile as he finished reading the notice.

There will be a funeral service for Drew Whittaker on Friday 12th March at 09h00 at the Waltham Abbey Church. Donations please requested in lieu of flowers to The Suicide Prevention Fund set up in his name www.Inmemoryofdrew.co.uk. Thank you for being a friend of Drew. We hope his memory lives on in all of your hearts.

Taylor closed his eyes as the sick feeling in his stomach threatened to overtake him. He fought it off and took a couple of deep, calming breaths. Drew's smiling face leapt up off the page. He and Drew went way back. They'd been occasional fuck buddies, mutual 'blow jobbees,' and had been jerking each other off for over a year off and on in the small hotel behind the music store. Drew was also a married man with two kids, whom he adored—or *had been* a married man, in any event. Taylor had never felt quite comfortable with being the "bit on the side" when the man had a wife at home, but Drew had assured that if not him, then it would be someone else. And he had really liked Taylor. That like had been reciprocated.

In his mid-forties, Drew had been a man so far in the closet that it would have taken him a week to get out of it. He'd been unrepentant about his need for younger men to give him the satisfaction he needed. Taylor and he had met at a grocery store and Taylor had instantly recognised the hunger in the other man's eyes when they'd stood at the vegetable stall talking about the best melons to buy. One thing had led to another, there'd been a quick BJ in the customer bathroom—Taylor on his knees taking Drew's big cock in his mouth and turning the man into a slush puppy—and the two of them had fallen into a comfortable rhythm of quick fucks and encounters to satisfy them both.

It had been no hardship for Taylor. Drew was a handsome man, slim and pumped from working out in his home gym, and Taylor had appreciated his considerable assets, especially when the man was pounding his arse. He'd also been a warm and generous lover and Taylor had even once thought that if Drew had been out of the closet, and not already attached, he might have considered a man like him permanently in his life. And now he was dead.

Taylor hadn't seen him since the last very tasty suck off about three weeks ago. He'd thought nothing of it; Drew was a businessman who travelled all over the world and there was no commitment between the two of them to meet up with any regularity. That was what mobiles were made for. Insta-fuck was a new buzz word in Drew's dictionary and Taylor had enjoyed being part of the conversation.

He stared dismally out of the window in the street beyond. He'd have to make a plan to go the memorial service. Drew deserved that much. At least he'd found the source of his nightmares. He still smelt the blood and shit in his nostrils, and felt the desperation permeating the air. He reached over and powered up the small netbook he kept on the table. With grim determination he began the search for local stories. Ten minutes later he found the news article.

Police were called in yesterday to the home of Drew Whittaker, 42, after neighbours reported hearing a loud noise. Mr. Whittaker was found dead in his study, at his home in Waltham Abbey, from what appears to be a self-inflicted gunshot wound. His wife and children were not in the house at the time but were told of his death and are currently being comforted by relatives.

A wealthy entrepreneur, Mr. Whittaker was well known in the city. His position as CEO and owner of his multimillion pound company, 'Whittcon Enterprises,' which specialised in the manufacture of computer chips for the digital market, was cemented in respect and admiration from his peers in the industry.

Foul play is not suspected. Investigations into Mr. Whittaker's death are continuing.

Taylor gave a shuddering sigh and leaned back in the rickety dining chair. He felt a sense of helplessness that he hadn't been there to soothe Drew with any demons he'd had. He'd never even known what he did for a living. There might have been no promises between them but Drew had still been a friend of sorts. His throat ached and he tried to hold back the hot tears that threatened to fall from eyes that felt gritty and sore.

"God, Drew," he murmured as he closed the laptop. "What the hell happened to make you so desperate? Surely there was someone you could have talked to? I would have listened."

He stood up and picked up his jacket and shrugged into it. Time to go to work before he was late and his boss Jemima gave him a tongue lashing. The music store was her pride and joy and she relied on her employees to hold the same passion for it that she did. 'Music Mayhem' was a place that Taylor really enjoyed working and he had no desire to jeopardise his position by being late. With a heavy heart, Taylor left the house and made his way to the tube station.

That night, after a day from hell at the office, he was glad to make it home and collapse into the dilapidated armchair in the lounge. Leslie wasn't home yet and Taylor was glad of the peace and quiet. He closed his eyes and laid his head back against the chair. He had a smoke then lit up another one. When he was done, he got the air freshener out and opened the windows.

He'd been relaxing for about half an hour when he heard the front door open and a whirlwind hit the entrance hall as keys were thrown onto the small table. There was the tread of footsteps and a waft of expensive masculine eau de cologne assailed his nostrils. Leslie was home.

"Tay? Baby, are you home?" Leslie appeared in the doorway. His trim, lithe body was clothed in very tight black and white plaid trousers, a form-fitting white button-down shirt, currently rolled up to his elbows, and his black matching jacket slung over his shoulder. A silver scarf was wrapped around his elegant neck. Taylor bet he was the epitome of office chic at the fashion house he worked as a trainee buyer, and he could only but envy Leslie's casual yet innate sense of dress style. Leslie, however, was not as conservative when it came to his time off, with his high heels, makeup, thongs and myriad of bright and striking clothes.

"I'm here," Taylor said wearily and sat up, running a hand through his curls and wondering whether the top of his head resembled a bird's nest in the making.

Blue lasers fixed on his face, a patrician nose sniffed the air in suspicion and then a worried frown crossed Leslie's beautiful features. Taylor was glad he'd been distracted from the stale cigarette smoke.

"Honey, have you been crying? Your eyes are all red and puffy, and you're as pale as my mum's tea. And we know all she does is dunk the tea bag in once and drink tea-flavoured dish water." He shivered, his face disgusted. He sat on the chair arm and laid a warm hand on Taylor's back. "What happened?"

Taylor sighed. He should have known he wouldn't get away with much when it came to Leslie.

"I had some bad news this morning and I had a shitty day. I sold something for less than I should have and had to make it up, and Jemima crapped all over me for it. Then I dropped a whole tray of drinks I was making on my tea round at lunch time, and coming home the tube was packed and some random guy goosed me." He closed his eyes at the gentle strokes of Leslie's hand on his back. "I wouldn't have minded, but he was dirty and smelly and I had to spend the whole journey with my nose in his armpit. And not in any way I normally like."

Leslie tut-tutted as he stroked Taylor's hair from his face. "Oh fuck. That does sound like a shit day." His eyes met Taylor's. "What was the bad news?"

Taylor swallowed. "Remember the nightmares and the blood? Well, I know who it was now. A friend called Drew. He shot himself."

Leslie gasped, his blue eyes wide. "Oh my God, sweetie, that's bloody awful." He scooted onto Taylor's lap as he sat in the chair and hugged him like a limpet. Taylor was grateful for the closeness even if he was being squeezed to death.

"What kind of friend was he? Were you two close?"

Taylor shook his head tiredly. "He was a fuck buddy. A good guy though, and he didn't deserve whatever he went through. I don't know why he did it."

Leslie's eyes clouded. "Baby, I'm so sorry. But at least it explains the visions you were having. That must be a relief, that you know what they were."

Taylor's throat clenched. "Until the next time when someone close to me dies or I see the pain of someone close to them as they die? I'm fucking fed up with this whole curse of being psychic. I wish I was just bloody normal."

Leslie pressed soft lips to his temple. "But you're not, sweetie," he said softly. "You're my Taylor and my hero. And a lot of other people's too. I don't claim to understand what you do, but you've helped people. Like me, and Eddie. And that little boy." In one of his darkest down moments, Taylor had told Leslie the story of little Bobby Meredith and they'd cried together over that tragic tale. "So you need to suck it up and put on your big-boy pants." He wrapped his arms around Taylor's neck and gave him another smacking kiss on his cheek. "I know just the thing to cheer you up. Chamomile tea. I'll go make you a cup."

He scrambled off Taylor's lap and sashayed his way into the kitchen. Taylor heard the soft tones of a song by Lady Gaga, Leslie's personal lady crush, being sung in a melodic tenor voice as Leslie rattled cups and filled the kettle. Taylor grinned wearily. Chamomile tea was the remedy for all the ills of the world according to his roommate, and just for once, he wished that the magic brew could take away the pain he felt at a friend's untimely death.

*****

A week later, on a cold and grey Wednesday afternoon, Taylor stood quietly at the back of the beautiful church in Waltham Abbey. He'd been lucky to get the day off work, promising Jemima that he'd make up the time. He was dressed in a sombre grey suit, feeling as uncomfortable as all hell. It was an outfit outside of his comfort zone, being more used to chinos, jeans and sweat shirts. Leslie had tsk-tsked and told him to get a grip when he'd complained the suit was tight across his shoulders and restricted his movement. When he'd continued whinging, Taylor had gotten a glare from his friend and an admonition that "someone was fucking dead, and Taylor could play nice in a suit for a little while."

He watched the people milling around as they talked softly and occasionally gestured to the coffin that sat at the front of the wide, ornate chapel. It was covered in myriad types of flowers and looking for all the world like a display at the Chelsea Flower Show. Taylor himself wanted a Viking funeral. He'd actually written it into his will two years ago, although the solicitor writing it had coughed gently and told him he didn't think the UK condoned putting someone on an old wooden barge and setting them on fire on the

Thames. Taylor had growled that it was his effing funeral and the powers that be could go screw themselves. And so the clause had stayed.

Writing a will at the tender age of twenty-two had been something that had raised eyebrows in the conservative offices of Lester, Mark and Abelard, where Taylor's father worked as one of the partners. Taylor, however, had seen enough death through both his and his mother's eyes and he knew that when the Grim Reaper came calling there was fuck all anyone could do it about it. He might not have a lot to leave anyone other than his collection of antique cigarette boxes and a pile of choice porn magazines, but he was damned if he was leaving what he did have to the State. He knew Eddie and Leslie would make good use of the magazines, the pages of which were already rather stuck together.

Taylor's chest tightened as he watched a pretty, dark-haired woman he knew to be Drew's wife place her hand on the coffin. Taylor had seen the pictures of Catherine, Drew's wife, when he'd taken them out his wallet to show him.

Drew had been proud of his family; there had been no doubt about that. The love for his wife and children had shown in his eyes. Another older man, probably Catherine's father, put a comforting hand on her shoulder. She was crying silently, her face grief stricken. This close to home, Taylor realised exactly what he'd done. He'd fucked and been fucked by a man who was already spoken for to another. His stomach churned with guilt. Drew *had* explained that he'd no other choice; he had needs he didn't want to share with his family and the occasional bout with Taylor was his way of unwinding.

At the time, Taylor had understood. But now, in the cold light of day, when said man lay cold in a coffin, and Taylor saw the grief of the family, he wondered whether he'd done the right thing in being there for Drew so others hadn't needed to be. He was glad that wherever Drew was, he wasn't in the church today. Taylor couldn't sense him, for which he was relieved. He felt it more at the time of the event, not afterwards. His mother had felt more than him, to the point of almost being haunted by past presences. It was probably what had caused her heart to give out at the relatively young age of forty-nine.

"Are you friend or family?" The gentle tones of a woman echoed breathily in his ear. Startled, Taylor turned to see a tiny, white-haired woman, in about her seventies, regarding him with bright, bird-like eyes. She was dressed in dark blue dress, a white shawl draped casually around her shoulders.

"Uhm, I was just a friend," he stammered.

She nodded sadly. "Yes, Drew was a popular man; he had a lot of friends. That's why it doesn't make any sense that he did what he did. I still don't understand ..." Her voice tailed off, her face whitewashed with grief. She lifted a soft, white hand to Taylor to shake. "I'm Lavinia Whittaker. Drew was my grandson."

Taylor shook her hand and wished the ground would open and swallow him up with the lie he was living. "Taylor Abelard, ma'am."

"How did you know him?" Lavinia asked, head cocked to one side like a little sparrow.

"He used to come into the music shop where I work." Taylor was glad that at least that was the truth. "He had a thing for a group called 'In Vitro,' an alternative group, and I used to keep the new releases for him to collect."

Lavinia grimaced. "I think I heard that playing in his car one day. Dreadful noise it was, all screeching and percussion. It made my ears weep blood." Her hand flapped and she looked quite disgusted. But there was a soft smile on her face—a memory perhaps of better days when her grandson was alive?

Taylor chuckled, liking the older woman. "It's not my taste either. I never quite saw what *he* saw in it. But he enjoyed it so I helped him find the albums he wanted." He shrugged. "It didn't take a lot to make him happy." No sooner had he said the words than he wanted to withdraw them.

It sounds too intimate, like I really knew him well. I need to be careful. I don't want his memories tarnished by a slip of the tongue. I have no idea if anyone knew about his other life.

Lavinia regarded him thoughtfully but said nothing. Instead she looked over at the woman still weeping at the front of the chapel, her face bleak and white. "Catherine has taken his death very badly. She was always very dependent on him and now she's a poor lost soul." She gave a deep sigh. "I hope her father can help her through this with the children. I've never seen someone so distraught."

Shame permeated Taylor's very soul. Soft strains of music filled the air and people began filling into the church.

"The ceremony's starting," Taylor said quietly. "Can I show you to your seat, Mrs. Whittaker?"

Lavinia laughed, a tinkling sound that made Taylor smile. "Oh, my dear, call me Lavinia, please. And yes, I'd love a handsome young man like you to escort me to my seat." She held out a thin, fragile arm and Taylor took it as he gently supported her to the front of the church pews. He helped her into the seat closest to the aisle and then turned to leave. She reached out and grasped his arm, her eyes slightly wet.

"He was a good man, one of the best. I'm glad he has friends here. I hope wherever he is now, he's at peace."

Taylor clasped her hand, thin and frail, between his dark ones. "I think he is, Lavinia. That's all we can hope for."

He turned and made his way to the back of the room, away from the family and the true friends that were Drew's. The ceremony was beautiful, heart wrenching and not over soon enough for him. It was with a sigh of relief that he finally went outdoors, found a shady spot under a huge oak tree and lit up a cigarette. He knew he'd promised himself to cut down or stop altogether but today? That wasn't going to happen.

"Those things will kill you, you know." The hated voice drawled in his left ear and Taylor swung around in shock to meet the deep, grey eyes of Draven Samuels.

"What the hell are you doing here?" Taylor growled. "Are you stalking me?"

Draven's face darkened. "Don't flatter yourself." He raised a hand and flapped the spiralling smoke from Taylor's cigarette away with disgust. Taylor blew a smoke ring in his direction in defiance and the man glowered.

"You are such a damn child." He regarded Taylor evenly. "I worked with Drew for a while. What's your excuse to be here?"

Taylor wasn't going to *ever* tell this man the real extent of his and Drew's relationship. "We were friends. He used to come into the music shop I work in." He noticed that Draven filled out a suit really well. Dark charcoal wool, suited to the chilly autumn days, with a pale blue shirt, which stretched across his chest and defined a body that was strong and toned. His blond hair was ruffled in the slight breeze and his face seemed paler than usual.

"No one should be here. It was too damn early for him to go. Stupid bastard."

Taylor's mouth dropped at the fact that a man who'd just died was being vilified. Draven squinted. "What? Are you into the whole 'don't speak ill of the dead' thing,' being in your profession?"

Taylor's temper rose with every word coming out of Draven's mouth but he wasn't prepared to make a scene at a man's funeral.

"You are a real shit." He blew another smoke ring toward Draven, noting with satisfaction as it hit his face and Draven's nostrils flared. "I don't talk to dead people, arsehole. That's not how it works."

Draven said nothing, just stared at Taylor with flat eyes. Taylor ignored him, watching the people walk out of the chapel and mill around, comforting each other. He caught Lavinia's eye and she waved. He waved back at her and blew her a kiss.

"You know Drew's grandmother?" Draven looked surly at that fact.

Taylor nodded airily. "Oh yes, we go way back. She's a lovely lady."

"Huh. I never heard her talk about you. Small world, isn't it, that we keep bumping into one another?" Draven's eyes were piercing and observing him with keen interest. And in their depths was a definite spark of interest. Taylor had seen that look often enough to recognise it for what it was. Lust. Desire.

Oh really? Mr. High and Mighty Samuels isn't above a bit of slap and tickle then with someone he doesn't really like. Interesting.

Taylor filed it away for future use. He shifted on his feet, thrusting his hands into his pockets and drawing attention to the front of his groin as the material tightened. Draven's eyes flicked down and his face grew still. His tongue came out and he licked his lips, and the sight of that pink muscle and the wetness of Draven's bottom lip turned Taylor's insides to mush as his cock began its inexorable rise upward.

Damn, that whole hands-in-pockets thing has bloody backfired on me.

He took his hands out of his pockets as nonchalantly as possible and pulled his jacket over as far as he could to hide the rise of the

Titanic under his boxers. Draven raised one very sexy eyebrow and smirked. Taylor wanted to slap it off his face. There was something about this man that made him want to get violent.

"So…" Draven drawled. "How does it work?"

Taylor was taken aback. "How does what work?" At first he thought Draven was talking about his cock but no. That couldn't be it.

"The whole 'I see dead people' thing. How does that work for you?"

Taylor tried to count to five to counter the fury welling up inside him. "I told you I don't see, talk or communicate with dead people." He said between gritted teeth. "I simply feel energies and see places in my mind where they might have been. And it's not just dead people I feel. It's the emotions of people close to me and who I have a connection with." He huffed. "So you needn't worry, because you'll never be one of them."

Draven chuckled sardonically. "Oh I think we have a connection all right." He motioned to Taylor's crotch. "Just not in the same way."

Taylor was dumbfounded. "Are you hitting on me at a bloody funeral?" he snarled. "You don't find that just a little bit sick?"

Draven shook his head. "Drew's gone," he said quietly and now Taylor could clearly see sadness in his eyes. "I knew him well enough to know that while he didn't want to live, he'd have no problem with the ones who did carrying on. He had a favourite quote: 'The life of the dead is placed in the memory of the living.' It's by Marcus Cicero. He'd expect us to remember who he was and the good times, not the one at the end who chose to take his own life." His eyes grew far away. "Some of us don't have that choice; we're still in limbo."

Taylor had the distinct feeling Draven was talking about something or someone else other than Drew. He also felt like a fraud. He hadn't really known Drew to the extent that he could take a favourite quote of his and tell someone about it. Draven had been closer to him than he'd ever been.

Suddenly the secluded copse of trees where Taylor had chosen to come for an illicit cigarette closed in on him. He needed to get away, away from the other man's knowing eyes and the breathless attraction he felt for a man who didn't even like him and considered him with contempt.

"I need to leave," he blurted and turned to go back to the car park, back to his car so he could get home and feel cleaner, to hide away and forget he'd ever come here today.

"You were one of his regulars, weren't you?" Draven's quiet voice made him stop. He closed his eyes in mortification but didn't turn around because he didn't want this man to see the shame on his face.

Draven kept speaking, his voice low. "I knew about Drew's proclivities and you're just his type." He stopped and Taylor stood stock still, not wanting to turn and see more contempt on Draven's face. "He was a noble man but in the end, he chose to leave this way instead of facing up to whatever it was made him do it." There was a short silence and Taylor took a step forward to leave. Draven's quiet voice stopped him.

"I think he was being blackmailed about it. Just a feeling I have."

At those shocking words, Taylor *did* turn around and instead of seeing disgust in Draven's eyes, all he saw was sympathy. He still needed to vent, though.

"Blackmailed for being queer? How do you get to that conclusion? And what the fuck do you know about me? The first time we met, you said I was a fraud. The second time around, you said the same thing. Now I'm a prostitute, a 'regular'? Well, fuck you, Draven Samuels." Taylor felt his eyes prickle with hot tears as emotions took him over and he continued his tirade with a cracking voice.

"I cared about Drew, and I'm really sorry that he's dead. I came here because I felt his death, his pain and I wanted to say goodbye and do the decent thing. Not something you'd understand." He felt a familiar lightness in his head and the panic that came with it. There were emotions running high at the funeral and he was picking up on them in his own heightened state.

I can't pass out again; I just can't be so damn weak. Damn this bloody gift, damn it to hell.

The world went black and once again in Draven Samuel's presence, Taylor slid to the ground.

*****

Draven cursed as the limp body of the younger man fell like a tree. He had just enough time to catch Taylor before he hit the hard, cold, pebbled surface. He heard a shout from over at the chapel and running feet. As he knelt down, laying Taylor flat and cradling him in his arms, one of Drew's other friends, Jim Carstairs, came running over, his face pale.

"My God, is he all right?" The man looked panicked at having yet another incident to manage. As if a funeral wasn't enough for one day.

Draven nodded. "He fainted, that's all. He's a bit overwrought. I'll take care of him. You get back to the family, Jim. Taylor here will be fine."

Relief crossed the man's face. "Oh, if you're sure, Draven. I'll tell Lavinia he's okay; she was worried about him. She says to bring him back to the house for the get-together." He turned and walked back to the chapel.

Draven looked down at the man who seemed to make a habit of fainting on him. He didn't think he'd been responsible for this one. It had seemed for a moment as if Taylor had gone somewhere, the pain in his eyes evident, and then simply shut off like a candle being blown out.

He patted Taylor's face gently, worrying about his pallor. He couldn't help but notice that the man wasn't as lightweight as he looked, that beneath that coffee-coloured skin was a man of substance, muscles taut and firm. And up close, he was even more beautiful that Draven had imagined. Long, dark lashes lying against smooth skin, full lips that were currently slightly open and very kissable, and curling hair that was the deep, rich black colour of ripe earth. A faint smattering of stubble beneath the classic lines of his nose and around his chin made Draven want to run his face against it. He looked like a decadent gypsy prince.

And isn't that fucking poetic. Get a bloody grip.

Draven scowled and continued his efforts to get Taylor to wakefulness. Finally, after a tap that had probably been a tad too hard, Taylor groaned and opened his eyes and Draven fell into them. Taylor's eyes were the colour of rich, baked toffee, with an emerald circle around the pupil, bleeding into the iris like emerald starbursts. The spell was broken when Taylor opened his mouth.

"What the fuck? What are you doing to me? Let me go." He started to rise and push Draven away.

Draven chuckled. "Calm down, your bloody virtue is safe, I swear. You fainted. Again. I'm going to start thinking it's me that has this effect on you."

"You wish." Taylor struggled to a seated position and looked around with dazed eyes. "Where's everybody gone?"

"Probably back to Lavinia's for the wake or whatever they call it. She said I should bring you there when you'd woken up."

Taylor shook his head vehemently. "I'm not going anywhere. I don't belong there. You can leave me and go on your own."

He rose, a little unsteady. Draven held his arm as they both got to their feet.

Taylor was pale. "Thanks for not letting me conk my head on the ground," he said grudgingly. "That would have been all I needed, a concussion." He dusted off his suit and grimaced. Draven still held onto him and Taylor looked over at him angrily. "I'm fine. You can let me go."

Draven didn't *want* to let him go. The nearness of the man, the scent of his cologne, the warmth of his body heat—it all added up to a sudden spike of want. Draven couldn't stop himself. He leaned over and crushed his needy lips over Taylor's soft, full mouth, revelling when it opened and Draven could get his tongue in there to taste the man. Taylor tasted of smoke and need and sin. When Draven finally drew back, his heart was beating as if he'd just run a marathon. He expected to be slapped or punched but nothing was forthcoming.

Instead, Taylor watched him with an expression of pure confusion and yes…there was definitely need and desire in those dark eyes. "I thought you didn't even like me," he murmured, his lips glistening.

Draven cocked his head. "I don't."

The next action gave voice to the lie in his soul as he pulled Taylor closer to him and took his mouth again greedily, like a drowning man gasps for air, and Taylor melted against him, his arms wrapping around his neck and holding onto Draven as if he was a life buoy.

When they finally pulled apart, both men looked at each other with eyes that asked a myriad of questions.

"This is crazy," whispered Taylor. "I…" His face darkened and he shot a look at Draven that made his body chill. "Oh, I see where this is going. I'm a 'regular' so you think you can take me home and fuck me? That I'm a cheap piece of arse? Well, screw you." His eyes glittered and before Draven could get a word in to refute that accusation, Taylor raised his arm and the next thing Draven knew, he was being catapulted backward by a fierce punch to his chin. As he staggered back and fell on his arse, Taylor loomed above him, the fire of a thousand flames in his eyes.

"I hope I never set eyes on you again, you bastard. Stay away from me." He turned and stormed toward the car park, leaving Draven fingering his aching chin and wondering what the hell had just happened.

A few hours later, after fielding some anxious enquiries from the people at the after funeral gathering about his bruised jaw, and eating more cake than he'd ever wanted to, Draven made his weary way to the Royal Hospital. It was one of his weekly visits on his way home to Charing Cross and while it distressed him every time he went, he couldn't miss visiting his little brother. He walked into the long-term care unit at the hospital and the nurse behind the desk greeted him warmly.

"Draven, it's good to see you again. How have you been?" Nurse Anita Richards was a stalwart in the unit, one of the long-standing devotees on the ward. She had looked after Jude since he was admitted nearly three years ago. She tut-tutted as she fingered the red bruise on his jaw. "Ran into something, did we? Or was that something obtained in the course of that secret job you do?" She clucked and Draven smiled faintly.

"No, someone got in a strop and decked me one. Not my finest moment. And it's fine, really. Nothing I haven't had before. How's Jude?"

Anita eyed him with compassion. "He's the same, as always. We're keeping him comfortable and fairly healthy despite the circumstances. Go on in."

Draven entered the quiet private room his brother "slept" in. His heart ached not for the first time at the sight of that pale, lifeless body, thin and wasted, eyelids taped down. Around Jude's slight frame, the machines that currently kept him alive and breathing whirred and pumped and whistled in a symphony of simulated living.

Draven sat down in the chair beside his brother and laid a hand against his cool cheek. Jude's light blond hair was wispy but well cared for, and his skin dry and pale despite the moisturiser that was constantly applied. He was a spectre of the lively, laughing boy he'd once been. His mother and father had always joked that Jude and Draven were carbon copies despite the age difference. They'd even sounded the same.

Draven's heart broke every time he saw him. "Hi, baby brother. I'm here, ready to read another story to you. We finished the other one last time, didn't we? Today we have…" he reached across and took the book off the metal side table, "*Christine*." He wrinkled his nose in distaste. Jude had adored Stephen King novels, and although a psychotic car hadn't been something Draven had ever wanted to read about, it had been one of Jude's favourite books.

Just over three years ago, Jude had been injured in the same accident that had killed Draven's parents. Jude had sustained severe head trauma when the out-of-control truck had careened into their car. Jude had been fifteen at the time, just two months short of his sixteenth birthday. Draven had been in the Ukraine on a case for Mortimer Investigations, ready to come back to the UK. It was the case where he'd met Drew Whittaker and his company, Whittcon.

Draven had rushed back to dead parents and a brother who the doctors told him was in a permanent vegetative state with no discernible brain activity and unable to breathe on his own. The machines keeping him alive were the thin line between life and death for Jude and one that Draven had never quite managed to sever. That line was all he had left of his family. He felt the guilt every day at not being there for them, at being on business at the time his whole family had been wiped out.

Sometimes, in his darkest moments, he wished he'd been in the car with them.

The only silver lining in the whole tragic tale was that his parents had left Draven a very substantial amount of money in both life insurance and wise investments. Every penny Draven had from that went to keeping Jude on these machines, and would continue to do so.

Doctor Frederick had talked about switching them off but Draven just couldn't do it. Not while there might be hope, something he clung to even though the doctors had told him quietly that there was none.

He opened the book and smiled at Anita when she came in to check Jude's airway, change his position to prevent bedsores, replace the tape on his eyes keeping his corneas healthy, physiotherapy, checking his catheter and other waste bags and several other functions that kept Jude comfortable and relatively healthy.

"He seems to be doing okay. Thanks for the cup of tea, by the way."

The nurse smiled gently. "You know we love to look after you, Draven. You look tired. You should get some more sleep. You'll have Sister Alison on your case if you don't."

The retort on Draven's lips that he'd get more sleep when he was dead didn't seem right under current circumstances. Instead he inclined his head.

"I'll do my best. I wouldn't want to upset Ally. She'd probably put me over her knee."

Anita nodded and left the room with a whish of starched white uniform.

Draven sipped his tea and sat there, watching, touching and talking, pretending that one day, Jude would open his eyes and everything would be all right in Draven's world once again.

He got home around about eight o'clock, exhausted, emotionally drained and feeling the effects of the punch to his jaw. Taylor had quite a right hook on him and was stronger than he looked.

After pouring himself a whisky, Draven slumped down into the easy chair in the lounge in his small but cosy two-bedroomed terrace house and stared at the wall while he sipped his drink. A picture of happier times of him, Jude and their parents laughing on a beach somewhere hung there.

"Evening, guys," he murmured softly. "Is it okay to tell you all about my day?" It was something he did when he felt down, feeling that perhaps somewhere, they might be listening. "Where the hell do I begin? I went to the funeral of a well-respected business colleague. Then, I saved a man from bashing his head in, kissed said man, who's the most annoying and volatile man I've ever met, and got punched in the face by… yep, you guessed it, the same man. Who's sexy as hell, I have to say. Then I had yet another conversation with your doctor, Jude." He frowned at the memories of the conversation about possibly turning off Jude's life support. "I just wasn't in the mood to discuss his thoughts tonight. I like Doctor Frederick but he can get all rational and sympathetic and that makes me feel even worse."

Jude's brain damage was so severe that it was a miracle he existed at all. His neural activity was virtually nil, and while Draven understood all the terms they threw at him, having done extensive research himself to try and find a miracle cure, he knew that a minimal Glasgow coma scale of three was a very bad thing.

Since the accident Jude had never opened his eyes, made a sound, moved by himself or given any indication that there was anyone still inside his damaged body.

"I know they have your best interests at heart and they all think there's no hope and I'm holding on because I'm a selfish prat…" his voice trailed off as he choked up, "but Jude, you're all I have left now." He waved helpless hands in the air. "I can't do this on my own. How the fuck do they expect me to make that kind of decision? How does anyone *do* that?"

Draven didn't cry often, yet thinking about his brother no longer being around made his heart ache and his eyes prickle. He sat, sipping his drink, then poured another one until he could think unpleasant thoughts no more and retired to bed.

It was the best place to be at times like these.

Chapter 5

Taylor sat in Galileo's at his corner table and picked at his plate of chicken wings. It was a quiet Tuesday night and he'd come there straight from work. The events of the week before had been on his mind and he'd spent the weekend mulling them over, having come to the conclusion that even if Draven Samuels was an arsehole, perhaps Taylor had misjudged the hot kiss at the funeral. Taylor had never punched another man before and he felt really bad about it. He'd once hit a pervert with a truncheon to save a friend, but in his book, that didn't count as anything to feel guilty about. So he'd tracked down Draven's telephone number via Gideon. Gideon, being the soul of discretion, had called Draven first to ask if it was okay to pass his number on. Taylor guessed he'd been happy with that from the smirk on Gideon's face as he'd handed it over, with Eddie grinning like a Cheshire cat behind him.

"What?" Taylor had said in irritation. "I just want to apologise to the guy for planting him one. Take that damn smug look off your face."

The conversation with Draven had been short and sweet. A quick "Hello, this is Taylor, I'm sorry for hitting you, I think I might have overreacted," was blurted out in a vomit of words, followed by silence on the other end of the phone.

"Ermm, okay," had been Draven's response, drawled out rather uncertainly. Then he'd spoiled the whole 'Taylor–being-the-bigger-man thing' by asking cheekily,' "Does this mean I get to kiss you again?"

Taylor's jaw had dropped and instead of telling the man to sod off, the next words out of his traitorous mouth had been "Would you like to have a drink with me at Galileo's tomorrow night?"

No sooner had he said the words than he'd been mortified. To his surprise, Draven had chuckled sexily, causing Taylor's nether regions to react in a way he didn't think boded well for said drink, and said he'd see him there at eight p.m. Tuesday night. Taylor had put the phone down feeling very unsure about what he'd just agreed to.

Now he sat, waiting for Draven to arrive. He'd been outside for a couple of smokes already, to fight of the nervousness. Once or twice he'd thought about eating up his snack and bolting out of the restaurant. He'd just made up his mind to settle up at the front desk and take the coward's way out when a familiar scent of a woodsy cologne hit his nostrils and a deep voice said,

"Evening."

Taylor swallowed the half-chewed piece of chicken he'd been busy with. It burnt as it went down his throat and he grimaced.

Shit. That's going to give me heartburn.

"Errm, evening. Please," he motioned at the empty seat across from him, "take a seat."

Draven did so, his usual scowl for Taylor replaced with one of the most charming grins Taylor had ever been the recipient of. His stomach clenched and his black Levi's grew tighter. The other man was dressed in an open–neck, deep wine-coloured shirt with long sleeves. It hugged his torso like a wetsuit, revealing a body that had definitely seen its share of gym work. Taylor had already noticed the rather chic-looking grey chinos plastered to the man's long, lean legs and the way they clung to his arse like a second skin. He wondered faintly if Draven knew how damn sexy he looked. That thought was confirmed when the waiter came over to take a drink order and deliver menus and Draven gave him a five-hundred-watt smile that seemed to make the teenager—well, he was eighteen at least—almost cream his pants and return the smile. The waiter fell over himself in his effort to impress Taylor's dinner partner and Draven fed off it like an incubus. Taylor scowled and played moodily with the stem of his empty wine glass.

Draven finished his drink order—a whisky on the rocks—and raised an eyebrow at him. "Not a fan of whisky then?"

Taylor frowned.

"You seemed to disapprove of my choice of beverage from that frown on your face." Draven's eyes glinted with amusement.

Taylor stared at him loftily. "I have nothing against whisky."

Draven's lips quirked.

Taylor ignored him as he turned to address the star struck waiter. "I'll have a rum and Coke please. Make sure it's white rum. I don't like the dark stuff. Bacardi would be fine if you have it."

Jim—Taylor had now seen the tag on the waiter's jacket—nodded but continued to smile at Draven who winked at him. Taylor's blood began to boil.

You're my *fucking dinner date, you moron. And Twinkie— you keep your paws off him.*

Where this sudden possessive instinct had come from, Taylor didn't know. He just knew that if Jim Boy didn't stop ogling Draven, he was going to have his eyes poked out with Taylor's fork.

I am going to fork you up, Jimmy, my lad.

He sniggered at that random thought and Draven pursed his lips, the amusement on his face plain to see.

"I'm glad to see you're in a better frame of mind than the other day." He poured a glass of water from the jug on the table. "You pack quite a powerful punch." He sipped the drink, his eyes regarding Taylor.

Taylor flushed as he fiddled with the cream napkin on the table. "Yes, I'm sorry about that. It was probably uncalled for and I suppose I should apologise."

Draven leaned back in his chair. "I wasn't looking for an easy lay," he said softly. "I just really wanted to kiss you. I can't explain it either but there you go."

"I wasn't really at my best," Taylor muttered. "You caught me off guard with knowing what Drew got up to in his 'secret' life." His tone sounded bitter even to him. "I was fine with what he was doing with me when he was alive, then I saw his wife and kids and…" His voice tailed off. "I felt like a slut."

Draven leaned forward and placed a warm, firm hand on top of Taylor's, stilling his fidgeting. "Drew thought very highly of you," he murmured." "He never told me the name but he did tell me about his beautiful, chocolate-skinned young man and I just knew it was you when I saw you at the funeral. You really made him feel special and he was very fond of you in his own way." He sighed and his thumb continued stroking Taylor's hand.

Taylor was holding his breath because having Draven doing that unconscious caressing was causing him to have one very extreme reaction in his trousers, not to mention the constriction in his chest that made breathing difficult. His mouth was dry, his skin warm and prickling with heat and Taylor wondered why the hell he was feeling this way toward a man he'd only met a few times.

"Drew would never have left his wife. And he said the times he spent with you made him feel whole. So whatever you're thinking of yourself, slutty certainly isn't a word I'd use." Draven grinned. "And he was right anyway. You *are* beautiful." His brow furrowed. "I know I've expressed some opinions about you in the past, and I still feel the same way to a point. I can't believe in things I can't see, and anyone that makes a living out of these so-called feelings and crap…well, it's just difficult to get to grips with."

Taylor pulled his hand away. He was still in shock at Draven calling him 'beautiful.' The warm glow that suffused his body from head to toe at that comment was still heating him up. "I don't make a living out of anything I've done," he said curtly. "I do it because they need me, not because they pay me." He laughed sharply. "Believe me, if I did I wouldn't be working in a music store nine hours a day, six days a week, and eating ramen noodles and tomato soup."

Jim arrived with the drinks and they fell silent as he busied himself with fussing over getting a coaster for Draven while he simply placed Taylor's drink on the tablecloth. With a smile and a promise, the young waiter disappeared.

"He is so hot for you," Taylor grumbled. "Doesn't he realise we're here together?"

Draven raised a sardonic eyebrow. "Oh? Are we 'together' then?" His lips quirked and he raised his whisky to them and Taylor watched as those full, pink lips wrapped themselves on the rim of the glass as he drunk. He swallowed.

"Well, we are here having dinner, so I guess that counts as being together. Don't get too full of yourself. This isn't a date; I just wanted to buy the man I hit a drink."

Draven nodded, his eyes sparkling. He acknowledged the comment with a tilt of his head. "Of course. Not a date."

Taylor bit back a rude retort as Jim appeared once again to take their meal orders. Taylor was surprised that the waiter didn't feel the waves of dislike emanating from him. Jim managed to brush Draven's shoulder with his hand every time he moved, leaned in to listen to Draven place his order like a man about to deliver a passionate kiss and finally bestowed a dazzling smile on him as he helped Draven tuck his napkin on his lap. Taylor's eyes narrowed.

Oh really? You needed to go there? *God, I need a smoke.* He glanced longingly at the pack on the table next to his lighter.

As Jim flounced off, Taylor glared at the table, wishing it would burst into flames and follow the young waiter like a table tornado, reducing him to a pile of ashes.

"Fuck. That is one mean look you are giving this table," Draven laughed. "I'm glad it's not directed at me. I'd be worried." He reached out and slowly traced his thumb across Taylor's bottom lip, his eyes dark and sultry. "There's only one man I want to kiss here. And it isn't Jimmy over there. And to be honest, kissing isn't the only thing I want to do to you."

The heated look in his eyes melted Taylor's reservations about anything this man might want to do to him or with him. He knew Draven wasn't very accepting of what he did but he seemed to be willing to listen at least. And at the moment, Taylor couldn't care less. He hadn't been laid in a while, the man was mesmerising, and sex was sex. He'd take what he could get and if that made him the slut he thought he was, so be it.

Out of the corner of his eye, he saw Jimmy approaching their table with a basket of bread.

I think it's time to give this little upstart some competition.

$$*****$$

Taylor leaned into Draven and ran a hand down the clean-shaven cheek, hearing him hiss at the touch. Jimmy stood before them, a look of sad, resigned surprise on his face.

"And what exactly *is* it that you want to do to me, Draven?" Taylor drawled, licking his lips and seeing Draven's pupils dilate in sheer satisfaction.

Oh yes, Jimmy lad, take notes. I'm the one doing that to him, not you. So piss off and leave us alone.

"God, you are one teasing little bastard." Draven's voice was husky and he shifted in his chair. Taylor smirked at the fact that he didn't even seem to see Jimmy at his side. "I guess my reply would be, what don't I want to do with you, Taylor? Perhaps we should leave and find out just how far we can get." Draven smirked back. "Do you think we'd make it to my car or will I be fucking you right here on this table?"

Jimmy gave a plaintive squeak and scurried off like a frightened rabbit. Taylor stared into grey eyes that held so many promises, and he knew he was irretrievably snared. Jimmy's impression of a scared cottontail had nothing on Taylor's desire for this man to possess him in any way he wanted, to hold him down, take him and use him.

The two men couldn't get out of Galileo's fast enough. Taylor left money to cover the drinks even as they argued over *who* would do it, and he hoped Gideon would forgive him for deserting their post before their food arrived. He *had* given Sarah on the front desk a rather garbled explanation about a family emergency as he'd exited the restaurant and "sorry for the mess up." Once on the pavement, he and Draven looked at each other.

"My place," Draven commanded. "Closer and more private. Get in the car." He waved towards an expensive-looking Honda Civic parked in a bay a few places down from the restaurant. He clicked a remote from his pocket and the car beeped. Draven slid into the driver seat, as Taylor slid in beside him, and they both fumbled with seatbelts.

Taylor tried to distract himself from the fact he was going home with this man to be fucked into oblivion. "Nice car," he said lamely. "How did you manage the parking space? They're like, really rare around here."

"I have a special permit in the window to park places I want to. No one messes with it. And the car is a tourer. Suits my work. Space and comfort all in one." Draven started the car and pulled out at a speed Taylor was sure wasn't legal.

"Where are we going?" He wondered if he should tell someone, perhaps Gideon, where he was off to in case Draven turned out to be a raving killer. Although Taylor was sure Gideon wouldn't let a man who was a little crazy into his cherished restaurant. He was reputed to be a good judge of character. Taylor grinned inwardly. But then Giddy *did* like Eddie…his thoughts randomly buzzed in his head like anxious dragonflies trying to escape a net. Draven's voice interrupted his musings.

"Charing Cross. I have a house there."

"Oh. Nice area. I'm in Kennington myself. Roebury Avenue." Taylor sat back and closed his eyes, willing the drive to finish before Draven killed them both. His fists clenched at his sides, his erection slowly deflating. He'd always hated fast cars and speed, ever since a close friend had died in a fiery ball after hitting an embankment speeding. Taylor had experienced it, felt Michael's agony and fear, and been incapacitated for the best part of the day. Now he felt as if he was reliving that event and the emotional toll was rising.

Draven drove like he seemed to live his life. No nonsense, take charge, efficient and fast. Risky and on a knife's edge. He didn't seem to notice Taylor, sick feeling in his stomach, gripping the leather seats with white knuckles, bracing his feet in the foot well, his body rigid with expectation and panic each time the car slew around a corner, or stopped sharply to meet the needs of a red traffic light. Taylor concentrated on his breathing.

In, out. In, out. In, out.

He was just starting to get the hang of this ride from hell when Draven shouted out a fierce expletive and the car shot out, going even faster. Taylor heard a screech of metal brakes. He couldn't help it. He shrieked like a girl and turned to Draven in fury.

"Hell, do you have to drive like a bloody maniac? You almost hit that guy!"

Draven turned to look at him in surprise and Taylor felt faint. "Look at the road. Please. Look at the damn road, not at me. Oh hell. I'm going to be sick. Stop the car. Stop the effing car."

Draven swore loudly. "Just hold on, I need to find somewhere to stop. Good Christ, what is it with you whenever we're together?"

A few seconds later, he'd pulled over under a streetlight in what appeared to (thankfully) be a fairly deserted road for London, and Taylor unclipped the belt, staggered out the car and was promptly sick into the rubbish bin attached to the light. When he'd finished hacking up the contents of his stomach, he stood up, dizzy and still nauseous.

Draven's eyes glinted in the dim light but his face looked worried. "Taylor, are you all right?"

"Oh, I'm just peachy fine, fuck you very much," Taylor spat in fury. "Who the hell taught you to drive? Stirling-fucking-Moss?" He held tight to the lamppost. "Oh wait; he's dead, isn't he. Well, one day you might join him if you keep driving like that!"

Draven rolled his eyes, which didn't help Taylor's temper. "Christ, you are such a prima donna. I knew this was a bad idea."

"A bad idea?" Taylor was hyperventilating now. "You're a bad idea. This whole bloody thing is a bad idea. I think you need to take me home." He patted his pockets, looking for a cigarette and groaning loudly when he realised he must have left them at the restaurant in his hurry to get out.

Draven moved forward, a look of resolve on his face. "No."

Taylor glared at him. "No? What do you mean, no? Who died and make you God?"

"Taylor, you're upset. My home is about five minutes away. Let's get back in the car, and you can calm down at my place. You can wash your face and brush your teeth." He gripped Taylor's arm, "Maybe have a shower and just chill out for a while." His face grew anxious. "Shit, do you need a paper bag? You're breathing very hard."

"And I'm not even coming," Taylor growled. "And that's not going to be on the cards either when we get to your place."

Draven shrugged but there was a hint of a smile on his face. "Fine. Let's just get there and you can stop going all kamikaze on my arse and perhaps we can salvage just a little of this night. What do you say?"

Taylor said nothing, just stormed off to the car, ripped the door open and plonked into the passenger seat. His mouth tasted like crap, his breathing had gone back to normal, and his body felt like it had been through a fast spin cycle in a wash machine. He glowered at the dashboard as Draven got in the car and buckled up.

"Go slow," Taylor muttered. "I don't like fast. Brings back bad memories."

Draven's eyes widened. "Shit, why didn't you tell me you'd been in an accident before? I wouldn't have driven like I did." He grimaced as he started the car and pulled out, very slowly and painstakingly. "With the work I do, we're all taught defensive driving and do advanced speed courses. I sometimes forget other people aren't used to it."

"I haven't been in an accident. It was someone else that died." Taylor was suddenly very tired and all he wanted was to sleep.

"I see." Draven's voice was quiet. "I'll go slower, I promise."

Taylor was woken what seemed just like a few minutes later by a soft voice in his ear.

"Taylor, we're here. Come on. Let's get inside."

Taylor yawned and stretched and clambered sleepily out of the car. They were in a quiet neighbourhood among a row of pretty terraced houses, and Draven climbed the few stairs to one at the end. He rattled some keys and the door opened.

"Come on in. Welcome to Chez Samuels." He disappeared inside as Taylor followed into the dimly lit hallway. A light was switched on and he winced as the brightness hit his eyes. He looked around. It was small, cosy, masculine. Minimally furnished, with a lounge at one side, a kitchen on the other and what looked like a cloakroom. Decorated in deep shades of aubergine, white and bronze, the whole house looked elegant and classic. Very unlike Taylor's little bedroom with peeling wallpaper, a broken faucet at the small basin and frayed carpets covered in various stains. He loved his home with Leslie but this one was in a whole new league. He groaned at that thought. *Leslie.* He hadn't called him to let him know he wasn't coming home tonight. Leslie would have a full diva queen strop if Taylor didn't let him know. He pulled out his mobile and sent off a quick text.

Won't be home tonight. Pulled and ready to rock and roll.

That should please his roommate–even if it wasn't strictly true. He had no intention anymore of putting out for the man in the next room despite the hot and heavy breathing action in the restaurant. The vomiting and making a fool of himself yet again had put paid to that idea.

He went into the kitchen and Draven turned to him and passed him a toothbrush still in the packaging.

"Here, the bigger bathroom is upstairs if you want to brush your teeth. Feel free to shower if you fancy. I can give you a pair of sweats and a tee shirt. I'll leave them in the upstairs bathroom."

"Way to tell me my breath smells," Taylor muttered sulkily.

Draven grinned. "Wow, aren't you just a ball of sunshine." He turned to the large pink pig cookie jar on his counter top. "Freud, what do you think? Shall we adopt him?"

Taylor looked at the pig jar in suspicion. "You named your biscuit jar after a psychoanalyst who was obsessed with sex? And really, who names their containers like that?"

Draven frowned. "Freud wasn't obsessed with it. He was an advocate of psychosexual development."

Taylor looked at him blankly. "There's a difference?" He chuckled as Draven stared him down. "Okay. I'm off to give these stinky teeth a brush. Uhm, I don't suppose you have any cigarettes here, do you? I'd love a smoke later…" His voice tailed as Draven raised an eyebrow. Taylor sighed in resignation. "Fine," he huffed. "I'll do without. Just don't blame me if I get all cranky."

That poxy eyebrow lifted even further and Taylor wanted to smack the face that owned it. But that was what had got him here in the first place.

Upstairs in the bathroom, after seeing the luxurious wet room, Taylor decided to have a shower. He was sticky and sweaty and noticed he had spots of sick down his front.

"Way to go, Tay," he muttered as he shed his clothes and started the shower. "How can any man resist you in this state?"

He brushed his teeth, stepped into the shower and lathered himself up. Hot, steaming water had always had a restorative effect on him, making him feel better, washing away the emotions of the day and making his soul cleaner. He revelled in the smell of warm, orangey citrus shower gel, and hummed to himself as he washed his hair. He thought he heard a noise behind him and peeked out the curtain, but all he saw was fresh clothes laid out on the chair on the other side of the bathroom. Despite his resolve not to put out, Taylor felt a slight sense of pique that Draven hadn't even attempted to get in the shower with him.

Finally he turned off the water, wrapped a towel around his waist and went into the adjacent bedroom to change. This was obviously Draven's room—dark, deep shades of blue matched with white and lime green, giving the room a rather nautical flair. A clock shaped like a ship's rudder ticked quietly on a far wall and here and there were small items of a nautical nature. A ship in full sail, a lighthouse and a pair of nautical rope doorstops lying carelessly on the floor. Taylor changed quickly, towelling his unruly hair dry then putting the towel back in the bathroom. When he stepped out into the hallway, he started at seeing Draven waiting outside.

"Everything fit okay?" Draven said softly.

Taylor nodded. "The trousers are a little long but they're fine. Thanks."

Draven eye-fucked him from his toes, up the length of his body and then finally came to rest on his lips. The air of desire emanating from the man was disturbing and playing havoc with Taylor's decision not to fulfil their earlier intentions. He knew *that* bloody mindedness had been nothing but wishful thinking.

His cock inflated slowly in his sweatpants like a rising periscope. He stood stock still as Draven inspected him. The air around them seemed to thicken and warm, much like Taylor's dick. He knew Draven noticed the tenting in the front and his teeth showed in a wide, predatory smile. That smile made Taylor's blood tingle, his backside clench and his mouth want to latch onto Draven's like a Bengal tiger on a succulent morsel of dinner.

"I like the tattoo," Draven murmured, waving a hand at the intricate pattern on Taylor's inside left wrist. It was a pattern of thin, finely drawn vine leaves, winding up along a central stem from the wrist to the crook of Taylor's elbow. He'd had it done about four years ago when he and a previous boyfriend had decided to be adventurous. Taylor hadn't wanted any garish colours, so he'd stuck with the soft grey and black tones.

Draven stepped forward and in one quick move, he slid his hands beneath the loose tee shirt and pulled Taylor toward him. Taylor gasped as his own groin met one equally as hard and the warm, strong hands on his skin sent shivers through his body. *'All thoughts of resistance are futile'* was the first thought that went through his mind.

God, I sound like someone from Star Trek. I need to get a bloody grip.

He loved the feeling of someone taking control of him, someone tough and sexy leading the way. He ached for a man strong enough to see what he needed, and not hold back giving it to him. He didn't want to take it too far but being held down, dominated, needed—that turned him on like nothing else in the world. He'd tried it before in his relationships—the few he'd had that had lasted more than a few weeks. The ones where his lovers hadn't left him quickly because he was a freak when he had his "episodes," as one taunting lover had put it, but never been quite satisfied. His partners had either been too rough or not rough enough.

"You smell like sex and spice," Draven growled as his mouth slid down Taylor's neck and he licked the skin like said tiger. "You drive me fucking mad, you know that. I don't know how you do this to me. Why I want you so damn much."

Taylor closed his eyes as the assault on his neck and jawline continued. He couldn't speak. Hot lips grazed his skin, biting, nibbling and then finally, when he thought he'd go mad from the constant contact, Draven's mouth found his and Taylor's knees buckled. Draven's arm around his waist was the only thing holding him up, he was sure. Never before had he been kissed like this, ravenous, hard, unrelenting as lips and tongue filled him, tasted him, sucked him in and swallowed him whole. When a hand reached into the waistband of his sweats and gripped his cock, Taylor cried out, the sound seeming to inflame Draven more as he stroked him harder and faster, sliding fingers and palm over the slippery essence that coated his dick and making Taylor's senses overload. He pulled his mouth away from the rapacious one that was devouring it.

"Draven, please. You're going to make me come like this," he gasped, as the hand pulled up, released, and stroked down even harder.

Draven's eyes were black, his lips red and swollen, a slight tinge of blood where Taylor had bitten him. "Then come," he demanded and slid another hand round to stroke Taylor's arse cheeks, pulling them apart and grazing his fingers over his hole. Taylor bucked in Draven's arms, his balls tightening, his cock feeling impossibly hard as he climaxed, wet streams of musky come covering Draven's hand, his arm and the inside of the once-clean sweatpants. Draven held onto his dick until he was spent, all the time pushing against Taylor's hole and even inserting a finger at his moment of climax.

"God, love to feel you tighten around my finger like that," Draven panted. "Just think about what it will feel like when I have my cock inside you. Oh God, you feel so damn good,"

He pushed his groin against Taylor, rutting against him then shuddered, and Taylor buried his hands in Draven's hair, holding him tight as his own orgasm took him. Finally they were still, standing in the hallway and supporting each other. Taylor with his sweatpants covered in come and Draven with a huge wet spot in front of his usual immaculate trousers.

"Oh, God, that was pretty awesome," Taylor muttered as he leaned his forehead against Draven's sweaty one. "Why the hell did I have a shower if you intended doing that?"

Draven chuckled." "Because you reeked of sick and no matter how much I wanted to kiss you, that wasn't going to happen the way your breath smelt." He moved back and swatted Taylor's arse. "Now I guess we clean up and maybe we can progress to round two."

"Round two?" Taylor said faintly.

Oh God, all my dreams have come true.

That predatory look crossed Draven's face again. "Oh yes. I want to be buried deep inside that pert arse of yours and I'm intending on doing that just as soon we can." He shivered. "I'm not sure how long I can hold out though. I need to clean us both up then we can start again. In bed this time if that's all right with you?" He leaned in and ran his tongue across Taylor's lips, then bit his earlobe. "So let's get rid of this sticky mess then we can get dirty again."

He disappeared into the bathroom. Taylor stood there, horny again and confused. This had all happened very quickly. For two men who supposedly didn't really like each other, they were doing a damn good job of concealing it. He also wondered mutinously if he looked like a bottom because Draven sure as hell seemed to think so. Never mind that he swung both ways and could just as easily be buried in Draven's tight arse. He might like being manhandled but he liked to do a bit of his own too. He heard a slight noise behind him and turned. It had sounded like a faint whisper or a swish of something soft against a wall. He frowned, seeing nothing there to explain the noise. The noise came again, slightly louder this time but he still couldn't make it out. He waited patiently, then, no longer hearing it, he went into the bathroom.

*****

Draven stared at his swollen, bitten lips and sleepy, satisfied eyes in the mirror. He peered closer, as if expecting to see someone else there. His clothes lay in a heap on the floor.

That little session in the hallway had been explosive, and Draven had actually come in his pants, something he didn't do often. Taylor was so damn sexy, with that tight body, coffee-coloured skin and lips that begged to be ravished. He grunted.

Ravished? What the hell am I, some lead in a bloody romance novel?

He grinned at himself in the mirror as he swooped warm water up from the basin on the cloth and cleaned himself.

God, I am so fucked. I have never felt this strongly about anyone before. Let alone a damned professed psychic.

In getting to know the younger man who was now in his bathroom, Draven's instincts had already told him Taylor Abelard was no charlatan, no fraud out to make a quick buck. He'd checked with his friends in the investigative services and they'd heard a little about the "kid with the weird ability to sense scary crap," as one of them had put it, but Taylor had never been paid for any of those services. And according to those sources, he'd quite a good track record in helping the local police at the Lambeth Police Station—one sergeant in particular, a man called Rick Grant, someone with whom Taylor seemed to have a personal connection.

Draven couldn't deny that a little bit of the jealous green man in him wondered just how good friends they actually were.

He saw Taylor behind him, his eyes dark and smoky, his lips puffy and well kissed. His eyes travelled down Draven's body in frank appreciation, lingering on the curve of his arse. Draven loved that appraisal. He turned around and beckoned to the basin. "There's a wash cloth in there if you want to clean up a little. I'm done." He waggled his eyebrows. "I'll see you in bed."

"You do know it's only just gone ten p.m.," Taylor observed drily. "Old man."

Draven snapped the wet wash cloth against Taylor's backside.

Taylor jumped and swore. "Bastard. That stung."

He glared at Draven and Draven looked at the pale pink welt against the soft caramel skin. "Count yourself lucky it was only a wash cloth." His voice was husky and he was already growing hard again. "I have other implements that can make much sexier marks on that gorgeous skin of yours."

Taylor's eyes grew wide as his gaze flicked to Draven's growing erection, the desire in his eyes evident.

I see you in there, my sexy sub. I can see right into your damn soul.

Draven wasn't big into the BDSM scene but he liked being adventurous and using some of the sex toys on offer. It was finding someone else willing to do so that was sometimes the problem.

Draven caressed Taylor's arm. "I'll kiss your boo-boo better when we get to bed if you like? Lick it better, even."

"Boo-boo?" The husky tone of Taylor's voice turned Draven on even more. "I take the old man comment back. You're actually a kid."

Draven smiled wickedly. "Believe me, sexy, what I'm going to do to you tonight will never make any programme under the watershed. That will be strictly triple-X rated."

He bounced out of the bathroom toward the bedroom, laughing softly at the complete lack of noise coming from the bathroom.

Hell, this was becoming fun.

In his bedroom, he turned back the covers, adjusted the lighting and made sure the condoms and lube were in his side drawer where he normally kept those and other more extreme implements should anyone choose to play. He was pretty sure Taylor would make a beautiful playmate. He got under the covers and gave a sigh of satisfaction. There was still no noise from the bathroom and he called out.

"Taylor? I'm lonely here. Get your arse into bed."

There was nothing. No response. Frowning, he clambered out of bed and went into the bathroom.

"What's taking so long—"" His voice cut off at the sight of Taylor sitting naked on the floor, arms huddled around his knees, a blank look in his eyes. He was shivering, his skin covered in goose bumps; Draven wasn't sure if it was from the cold or something else.

"What's happening? Did you slip?"

Taylor continued to stare blankly into space, and Draven reached up and took a fluffy towel off the rack. He draped it over Taylor's shoulders as he tried to get him to stand up.

"I don't know what's going on, but you need to come out of here and into the bedroom where it's warmer, 'kay? Come with me. Get up, that's right." Slowly he lifted Taylor to a standing position and then led him into the bedroom.

Taylor was mumbling quietly now, words that Draven couldn't make out. He managed to get Taylor on his side on the sheet then pulled the covers over him. Still Taylor stared into blank space. Draven felt a prickle of fear down his spine. Taylor's eyes were vacant, glassy. He had no idea what to do other than let him get over whatever it was he was doing. He got into bed behind the shivering man.

"I'm here, just relax and sleep. I don't know what you're going through but I'm here." He leaned back and switched off the light. "I'm here for you. Sleep now." He wrapped strong arms around the chilled form and stroked Taylor's hair softly. All thoughts of sex had gone, and all Draven had left was a fierce desire to protect the man in his bed. After a while, the sound of deep breathing echoed in the still room. Draven leaned over, careful not to disturb Taylor and saw long eyelashes framed against pale cheeks. He felt a sense of relief as he lay back and pulled the covers up over them both again. Perhaps in the morning he could explain what the hell had happened.

Chapter 6

Draven awoke to an empty bed and silence. He blinked sleepily and
sat up in bed, the sheets falling to his waist. The house was still;
outside he heard the distant sounds of children playing. He swung
his legs from the bed and sat there, rubbing his eyes. He picked up
his phone and squinted at the display. Eight a.m. Christ, he'd slept in
for a change. Normally at between five and six-thirty without fail
he'd be waking up and padding through to the kitchen to make his
first cup of black coffee. He stood, stretched, yawned, pulled on a
pair of old sleeping shorts and went in search of Taylor. He hoped he
was still here and hadn't slipped out like a thief in the night. He was
disappointed. The house was empty of another human presence.

Draven swore. "Fuck. That little bastard."

His pique at last night's date and sex partner running out on him
caused him to storm into the kitchen and grab for the kettle. He
frowned. The kettle was still hot, which meant Taylor couldn't have
left all that long ago. He cursed again and reached into the cupboard
for a mug. He started as cold hands wrapped themselves around his
naked waist and the cup dropped just short of falling to the floor as
he managed to keep his grip.

"Did you miss me then?" Taylor sounded like he was smiling,
although his voice sounded a little…lost? Draven couldn't stop the
sudden pounding of his heart, both from fright and from—something
else.

"I thought you'd bailed on me," he said, his tone surly as he
busied himself making coffee, not even bothering to turn around.
The low, husky chuckle made his skin tingle.

"I heard what you called me." Fingers made light trails against
Draven's spine and he shivered. "I needed a smoke. Had to rush out
to that corner shop and buy some." Smoky breath blew against the
back of his neck and Draven's needy skin rose in goose bumps. Soft
kisses dotted the puckered skin, making him groan softly as he
closed his eyes and leaned back into the hard frame behind him.

"You know those things will kill you. Have you ever tried
giving them up?"

Great, here he was with a sexy guy kissing his shoulder and
caressing his stomach and all Draven could think to talk about were

his lover's smoking habits. The National Health Service would *love* him. Maybe they'd make him their poster boy.

"I did for a while. Then crap happened and I started again." Draven sensed the shrug. "We all have to die some way, right?" Taylor's voice was uncertain and his fingers ceased their soft stroking of Draven's midsection.

Draven's lower section was pretty needy, too, and the shorts he had on were no barrier to his rising cock, which was currently pressed against the hard surface of the kitchen counter. Draven shifted, trying to get some release. He didn't want to turn around, wanted to stay here all day with those fingers touching him, that unique scent of Taylor drifting into his nostrils, his breath warm and not unpleasantly fragranced. Draven didn't mind a man's cigarette breath; he found it quite a turn-on actually. And now he'd definitely *lost* any chance of being the spokesperson for the anti-smoking bods.

"That doesn't mean we have to give it help," he murmured and let out a gasp as a wet tongue slid into his ear then gently bit his ear lobe.

"Stop preaching. I get enough of that from Leslie. You're supposed to humour me."

Taylor's hand had now found Draven's cock, although admittedly it hadn't been hiding very well, and his fingers slid into the shorts with an easy move. He grasped the hardened, heated flesh that was trying to get out. Draven gave up all thoughts of making coffee or trying to make the world a safer place for non-smokers and yielded to that hand, pressing his arse back against Taylor's groin, finding him as hard as he was.

Both men were panting, small groans of satisfaction, need rumbling up for chests that were tight from lust and want. Taylor's breath on his ear and cheek was an aphrodisiac; his slight moans and throaty noises making Draven want him even more.

There was not much finesse in this early morning jerk-off; just strong fingers wrapping themselves around his engorged and slippery dick, stroking, pulling and gripping until Draven's balls shot up into his groin like steel marbles and he cried out, a soft, sharp expletive that shattered the earthy silence of the kitchen as he jetted hot, viscous fluid into his shorts, onto Taylor's hand and his own stomach. He leaned back against Taylor, legs weak with the force of his orgasm, and soft lips found his in an awkward embrace that left

Draven even weaker. He even thought he mewled like a kitten as Taylor's wicked tongue sank into his mouth, teeth clicking against teeth. Soft stubble left a burning sensation on his chin.

Finally they released each other and Taylor stepped back, allowing Draven to turn around and see him for the first time. There had been something so utterly hot about not yet seeing the man with his hands around his cock, simply taking what he wanted, giving what was needed.

Taylor stood, soft smile on his roughened, pink lips, eyes as dark as black holes, dressed in Draven's too-long sweats and an old Iron Maiden tee shirt. Those strong arms that had wrapped themselves around his waist were covered in faint, dark hair. His hair was wind- swept, curling in tendrils across his face, a face that regarded Draven with a mixture of satisfaction and apprehension.

There was something else too, a sense of unease emanating from the man. Draven wondered if the early morning hand job had been some sort of penance for something.

"You did something for me and I zoned out last night, and didn't get a chance to give you anything back, so…" Taylor lifted his shoulders in a Gallic gesture that Draven had seen on waiters in fancy French restaurants. An expressive shrug. He also felt a sense of disquiet that Taylor seemed to be able to read his mind.

"I didn't do it to get something in return," he said quietly, conscious of the sticky mess in his shorts and that he'd need another shower or at the bare minimum, a clean-up. "And yes, I was rather worried about you last night. I couldn't get you to wake up, or whatever."

Taylor's eyes narrowed. "It happens sometimes, you just have to let it run its course." He moved over to the cupboard and took another cup out. He switched the kettle on again and took Draven's mug from him. "Let me make this while you clean up."

Draven stared at him then glanced down at the bulge in Taylor's pants. "I can sort that out for you if you like," he said softly, but Taylor shook his head.

"No, I'm okay. Thanks anyway. I need to be off soon, back home." He gestured to Draven's busily whirring tumble dryer. "Hope you don't mind but I got up early and washed the vomit out of my clothes. I popped them in to dry, so they shouldn't be too long now."

The drying cycle was nearly over and Draven knew that particular one took two hours. "You must have been up early to wash them and get them in the dryer," he said, with a keen look at Taylor. "What time did you get up?"

Taylor busied himself spooning coffee into cups. "I woke up about three a.m., couldn't sleep so got up." He sounded tired and disheartened, his mood changing like the sun disappearing behind a cloud.

Draven reached out and grasped Taylor's wrist, his thumb caressing the tattoo. "What happened last night? One minute you were fine, the next you were in a kind of coma on the bathroom floor. Is that how it happens…these visions of yours?"

Draven knew how it worked on the television when people had psychic abilities. They either went all blank and white marble-eyed and spoke in funny voices, or their damn heads twisted around on their shoulders—something he found exceptionally creepy. He hid his face every time he saw a scene like that. Others simply went all Zen-like and creepy and he thought Taylor might fit into *that* category if that was what had happened last night.

Taylor gave a curt laugh as he poured water into the cups and then went to Draven's fridge to look for milk. The man looked really at home here. "Sort of. It's a bit like an out-of-body experience. You know you're around somewhere but you can't do much to communicate to the outside world.

"I knew you were there, by the way. Thanks for just getting me into bed and holding me. That was the right thing to do." He finished making the coffee, stirred both cups a few times then handed one mug to Draven. Draven took it, cradling his hands around the steaming coffee-fragranced manna from heaven. He took a sip and gave a satisfied sigh.

"God, that's good. I needed that." He glanced at Taylor. "So what did you hear or see in that sexy head of yours last night?" Knowing he'd probably get another punch to the jaw if he mentioned anything about Taylor seeing dead people, he tried to rein back the natural instinct he had to ask. He might be slowly and grudgingly accepting that perhaps Taylor did have something special now he was getting to know the man, but that didn't mean he understood any of it.

Taylor's eyes became wary. "Nothing, really." Draven knew he was lying. He was trained to spot them and this was definitely a liar in front of him. "I sometimes remember, and sometimes not. This is one I can't recall."

He sipped his coffee and Draven could see that in Taylor's mind, the questions were over. But he hadn't finished. Draven's co-workers didn't call him "The Inquisitor" for nothing.

"You're lying," he observed and drank his coffee, keeping his eyes focused on Taylor's face, which, predictably, grew mutinous and dark.

"I'm not fucking lying." Taylor slammed his coffee cup down on the counter, causing it to slosh over. Draven raised an eyebrow at the temper tantrum. He watched as Taylor went to the dryer and opened the door, stopping it mid cycle.

"It hasn't finished the cycle yet," Draven observed mildly.

"It's fine. They're dry enough for me to go home." Curt words were snapped at him like wet towels and Draven sighed.

"Taylor, come on, for God's sake. You scared me last night. One minute I'm expecting the blow job and fuck from heaven, the next I have a comatose man in my bed. Surely you know I'd be curious about what went down last night. And it wasn't you. "He tried to joke about it in the hope Taylor might lighten up. Instead he got a face full of angry man, a man like a spitting tiger cub, all claws and teeth.

"I gave you what you wanted earlier," he snarled. "I'm sorry I didn't manage to come to bed last night so you could fuck my arse, but I had stuff in my head to deal with, you tosser."

Taylor's teeth were bared, his hands balled in fists at his sides, but Draven saw the panic in his eyes. The man looked fraught, outwardly composed, but inside he was a damned mess.

Draven knew how to deal with this side of Taylor Abelard. He took hold of Taylor's arms and pushed him backward, towards the wall, pinning him there. Draven's hands tightened like steel bands on the other man's wrists, pushing them up above his head. Taylor tried desperately to break free but Draven knew his heart wasn't really in it despite the fire in his eyes. He'd seen the submissive side to this man, the man who ached for someone to take control. If ever there was a time to bring that side out, then this was it. Perhaps it would mean no more pissed-off psychic for a while.

"Let me go." Taylor's teeth grated between thin lips and Draven smiled. This seemed to inflame Taylor more as he struggled harder to break free.

"Nuh-huh. You, my friend, are going to listen to me instead of getting all pissy." His own body pressed against Taylor's and the flare of need in Taylor's eyes told him everything he wanted to know. Draven held his wrists, loosening his grip so as not to leave bruises. He brought his lips close to Taylor's, hearing him draw a shuddering breath, his cock stiff against Draven's rapidly hardening one.

"Something is worrying you. You went strange last night and whatever it was, it's unsettled you. You need to tell me about it so I can help you deal with it."

Taylor's amazing eyes stared into his and Draven's heart stuttered at the pain in them.

"I can't tell you," he whispered brokenly. "I don't really understand it all but I don't think it's good news."

Draven's spine tingled like an ice cube had been drawn down bare skin. Taylor bit his bottom lip and Draven wanted to kiss it. There was something about this man that definitely brought out the protective streak in him.

"Tell me," he whispered gently, relaxing his hold on Taylor's wrists. He knew Taylor wouldn't try and get free.

"I only dream, have visions about people close to me who have died or who may be in danger. Last night…." His voice shook and he closed his eyes.

"What about last night? Tell me," Draven demanded.

Taylor's eyes opened. "I dreamt about you." His voice was shaking. Draven leaned in, his lips brushing Taylor's cheek and he tightened his grip, wanting to make Taylor feel just how alive he was.

"I'm not dead, as you can see and feel. Nothing's going to happen to me. Although I'm glad you care just a little bit about something happening to me. There's hope for us yet."

Despite his tone of affected nonchalance, Draven couldn't help feeling a frisson of fear in his stomach. He supposed ruefully that was a definite sign that he was beginning to believe in Taylor and the voices in his head.

Taylor stared into his eyes with pupils as black as lava stones. "I heard your voice, or what sounded like your voice. You were asking me to let you go, to free you. You sounded so sad, and yet so yearning. I felt you all around me when you spoke, could smell your aftershave, feel you."

His voice grew fiercer. "I'm tired of this whole thing. Tired of feeling fucking scared and worried about what I see, tired of seeing people I know die horribly in my head, seeing mutilated kids in fields and smelling the blood. Oh God, Draven, when I smell things…" his voice tailed off and he closed his eyes in apparent exhaustion. "I just want it to stop. I want to be normal. I don't want anything to happen to you even if you are a pain in the arse." His breath hitched and Draven let go of his wrists and pulled him against him, wrapping broad arms around him. For a moment he held the firm body in his arms and listened to Taylor's soft breathing as he pressed his face against Draven's chest.

"Listen. Nothing is going to happen to me. I'm too bloody mean to die." Taylor's body tensed in his arms and Draven held him tighter. "And you know what they say? Only the good die young. And I am nowhere near good. Well, unless you count good at sex, of course. I'm pretty good at that, I have to say." He was warmed by Taylor's slight chuckle and snort. "So promise me you'll stop bottling it all inside and tell me how you feel."

He stopped as the enormity of those words drenched him like a cold shower.

Oh. My. Fucking. God. Since when did I become the sensible one in this relationship? I need to check I haven't grown girly parts.

Draven wasn't quite sure whether it was the thought of growing lady's bits or the fact he considered himself to be in a relationship that made his heart thump like a jackhammer.

God, we haven't even had proper sex yet.

These thoughts whirled around in his confused head and it was only when he felt Taylor shift beneath him, grinding his groin against his own erection that he came back down to earth.

He swallowed as Taylor lifted his head and gave him a searing hot glance from beneath sooty, wet-fringed lashes.

"Do you *want* to have proper sex?" The husky timbre of his voice went straight to Draven's cock, which perked up even more at those words.

"Oh. Did I say that out loud?"

Taylor nodded, amusement in his eyes. "You did, yes." His lips brushed Draven's, causing a jolt of electricity down his spine, and once again Draven wondered who had the power in this relationship.

Taylor leaned in and whispered, "Do you want to go back to bed and fuck me?"

"Is that a trick question?" Draven growled, releasing Taylor's wrists and then rubbing them gently. Taylor watched the slow movements of Draven's fingers on his skin as Draven traced the path of one of the vines on his wrist.

"Much as I'd like to take you up on the kind offer, I have to be at work in an hour or so for a meeting." Draven had never hated his job as much as he did now with a willing man in his arms and a raging boner. "So I'm afraid the proper sex thing will have to wait."

He brought Taylor's wrist up to his lips and kissed it lingeringly. Taylor's eyes watched every move. "So the plan is now I get in the shower… alone," he said decisively, even if he didn't want it to be that way. Taylor would be too much of a distraction and he'd never make it out of the shower. "Then I can get cleaned up and get to work before my damn boss fires my arse. He's not too happy with me at the moment anyway so I can't chance my luck. And you… you can stay as long as you want, and just lock up when you go. Chuck the key back inside through the mailbox. Do you have to be at work?" He raised an eyebrow and Taylor shook his head.

"I called in and took a personal day. I have some things to do today and I haven't had a day off in forever so they can do without me. My boss wasn't too chuffed about that either but she can go to hell. I'm never sick and I'm always there." His beautiful face contorted into a fierce tiger-cub frown and Draven thought it was adorable. "It's been a rough week and I need some me time."

Draven reached over and drew him in for a long, sexy kiss that made his own toes curl and the boner he was sporting even harder. He'd have a bit of work to do in the shower before he got out. Finally he pulled away, leaving Taylor with wet lips and dazed eyes.

"Right, I'm off to shower." He turned and walked toward the stairs. He turned back, a slight fluttering in his stomach preceding his next words. He had a visit planned, as usual, to the hospital to see Jude. He hadn't been as often lately due to work and personal commitments and he felt as guilty as hell.

"Errm, I have somewhere to be after work for an hour or two then I'll call you later. Don't phone me; I won't have my phone on where I'm going." Curiosity flitted across Taylor's face but Draven wasn't ready to tell him about Jude. Not yet. "And remember, nothing bad is going to happen to me." He winked at Taylor. "Keep that thought about the proper sex bit. I'll hold you to that later."

He felt Taylor's eyes on him as he walked up the stairs to the bathroom, and for once in his life, he prayed to whatever entities resided above and below that he could keep that promise.

Chapter 7

Taylor had no idea how he made it through the next few weeks without physically combusting. The spark that had ignited between him and Draven had become a raging furnace and neither of them seemed able to keep their hands off one another. He had no idea what this thing between them was. Taylor was disparaging of the whole "love at first sight" thing but he had to admit he hadn't felt this strongly before about a man who, in truth, he barely knew.

Taylor had been relieved that whatever the vision was that he'd had that night he'd first slept with Draven hadn't come to anything. He still heard the voice sometimes, soft yet yearning, but he'd learned to simply accept it as he did with others. It was more difficult to do, though. The *faux* Draven (because if he imagined it to be the real one he'd go bat-shit crazy) had felt helpless, and the yearning to be somewhere else had been all-encompassing.

Their days consisted of each of them at their respective jobs, keeping in touch with texts and quick phone calls. The nights—they were what held Taylor together. Long, passionate evenings into the early mornings, volatile sex and steamy shower sessions that left them both spent and exhausted. Most of the time they spent at Draven's house, as it was more private than having Leslie coming home, sometimes with a friend of his own. Taylor was feeling a little guilty about neglecting his friend.

Now, on one of his rare days off, he got up around eleven a.m. and stumbled tiredly into the small shower. After drying himself, he put on old tracksuit pants and a tee shirt that he grabbed from the wash hamper. It was close to one p.m. when, after checking his texts and emails—Leslie had texted him earlier from work saying he was staying the night at a friend's—and fixing himself a snack of peanut butter and jam sandwiches, he was seated comfortably in the old armchair with the remote, selecting a Netflix film called *Going Down in La-La Land*. He thought it sounded good enough to keep him occupied, and perhaps he might even engage in a little under-the-cover action later to relieve the permanent sexual tension he had.

Taylor woke up hours later, dry mouthed and needing to pee. He struggled out of the chair, wincing at the tired muscles and dried come on his stomach and took his trip to the bathroom. He rinsed his mouth out with breath freshener, cleaned himself up and loped tiredly back into the lounge. The afternoon sun shone in through grimy windows and Taylor thought not for the first time that he really needed to get around to cleaning them sometime.

After pottering around and doing some much needed housework he settled in to watch some television, glancing at his watch and wondering when Draven might call. It was close to eight-thirty p.m. when his mobile finally rang. His stomach dipped at the thought it was Draven. It wasn't him on the phone but he smiled when he saw who it was.

"Eddie, my man. What's up?" If he hadn't had the caller ID he'd still know who it was from the sounds of the kitchen in the background. Men's voices, the clutter of utensils and whir of whatever culinary machines made those sort of noises. Taylor wasn't big on the whole cooking thing.

"I should be asking you the same question." Eddie laughed. "How are things going with Mr. Blond and Grouchy? Are you still getting laid regularly?

Taylor smiled. "I can't keep up with him; the man is insatiable. But I'm enjoying his company." He wandered into the kitchen and took out a beer, uncapping it and taking a deep drink.

"Is he still being so bloody secretive about where he goes when you can't get in touch with him?" Eddie sniffed. "Are you sure he hasn't got another boyfriend somewhere, Tay? You know how I worry about you…"

"No, I don't think that's it," Taylor muttered. "He's hiding something, that's for sure but I don't think it's another man. The guy couldn't possibly do what he does with me and have a bit on the side, believe me. He'd have to have the stamina of Superman."

Taylor felt a twinge of discomfort at his own words. He'd been there, been the bit on the side and who knew just how much sex Drew had been getting with his wife before coming to Taylor? He supposed he shouldn't really make such wild assumptions.

"Have you asked him? You know, talked instead of just screwing each other's brains out?" Eddie sounded worried.

"Yeah, we talk. A little anyway, but it's more physical at this stage I think. He's a tough guy to get to know, but I really like him. He's a real softy inside; it's one of the things I like about him."

"Really? You mean that whole douche-bag thing he has going for him isn't the real Draven? Wow, miracles never cease." Eddie's teasing lifted Taylor's spirits a little. He also felt the need to defend his new lover.

"Oh, when you get to know him a bit better, I guess he's not such a bad bloke." Taylor tried to change the topic away from his sex life. "Anyway, if I recall Gideon used to be a douche bag too before you got your hands on him."

There was a loud snort from the other side. "Oh yeah, too true." Eddie's tone turned wicked. "You just need to train them then they become a little more bearable." His voice got louder and Taylor grinned as he realised Gideon had probably just walked into the kitchen. "I mean, what's the point of having a man if they don't toe the line and let you show them who's boss?" There was a yowl from the phone. "Ow, baby, that hurt. Really, you need to remember we're not in the bedroom now—you need to have some self-restraint. Ow!"

Taylor chuckled loudly as Gideon came onto the phone. "Tay? My man is having a sudden crisis this side; he says he'll call you later. I need to take him home and make sure he knows who's the boss." His voice was amused and loving and Taylor felt a pang as he realised how lucky Eddie was.

Will I ever have that someone who talks about me like he really cares? Is it going to be Draven or is that just a one-time thing?

The phone was obviously grabbed away as Eddie reappeared, breathing fairly heavily. "Damn bully. I'm back. Anyway, where were we? Oh yeah, I was asking you about your love life. Don't let the grass grow, yadda, yadda. And have fun, Tay." His voice grew serious. "Don't let him hurt you. He doesn't sound like the type of guy who's into relationships so make sure you don't get in too deep unless you know it's going somewhere. I did some checking on this guy and he's a bit of a player." Taylor had no illusions that Gideon had been Eddie's information source.

"So was I, Eddie," Taylor said softly. "I might not have brought a lot of guys home to the house when we stayed together but, believe me, I've had my fair share of casual sex." He remembered Drew and the warm light in his eyes as they'd lain in bed together. That hadn't really been casual to him.

"Thanks for worrying but I'll be fine. This thing with Draven isn't really serious. I'm not sure where it's going. Just a bit of fun really." He'd say anything to put Eddie's mind out of protective mode. He was tired of having everyone see him as someone who needed babying. Leslie had said much the same thing as Eddie.

He heard a noise at the kitchen door and turned swiftly to see Draven standing there, his face blank but with a strange look in his eyes. Taylor's heart leapt as he motioned to him to come in. Draven nodded and moved into the small space, crossing his arms across his chest and regarding Taylor evenly.

Taylor swallowed, feeling strangely guilty at his last words about Draven being a bit of fun. "Listen, Eddie, I need to go. Draven's just arrived, so I'll call you later in the week, okay? Maybe we can make a plan to go out for a beer, you, me and Leslie. Like old times."

"No worries. I'll speak to you soon. Oh, and Taylor?" Eddie's voice lowered to a whisper. "Fuck his brains out." The line went dead and Taylor laid his phone down on the side table and looked up to stare at Draven.

"Do you always leave your front door open?" Draven asked quietly. "Anyone could have come in. I did knock but you were occupied." For the first time Taylor noticed the brown folder under his arm.

Taylor shrugged. "You know I don't lock it when I'm home. It's not a bad neighbourhood. Maybe I should start, seeing as how just anyone could walk in." He smiled, meaning it as a tease, but Draven's jaw tightened and he cricked his head from side to side as if loosening tight muscles.

Taylor swallowed. "I wasn't expecting you to come over in person. I thought you were going to call first, like usual. Did you get your business sorted out, you know, the stuff you do after work?" Taylor didn't want to be nosy but it was a habit that was hard to break.

Draven nodded, rather curtly Taylor thought. "Yes."

He said no more but Taylor saw an expression cross his face, something sad and rather unsettling. He looked at Taylor, a wary expression in his eyes.

"Sorry, I didn't mean to walk in on your private conversation. I don't want to interrupt if you have plans." He uncrossed his arms and took hold of the folder in his left hand. "I should go. Maybe this was a mistake coming here unannounced."

Taylor frowned. He didn't want Draven to leave. "I told you that's not a problem. I come over to yours without always calling first."

Draven drew a breath. "I guess. Is it all right then if I stay?"

"Yeah, of course. I'll get you a drink. Beer?"

Draven nodded and Taylor fetched a San Miguel from the small fridge.

Draven scowled slightly. "So that was Eddie? What was he doing? Checking out what my intentions were toward you? Finding out how much *fun* you were having with me?" There was a slight bite to Draven's words and Taylor's stomach plummeted.

"So you heard the last part of my conversation then?"

Draven didn't reply but the way his nostrils flared told Taylor he definitely had.

"It's the only way to keep him off my back." Taylor explained, fairly lamely he thought. "He's not sure you're the right person for me to get involved with, and telling him that will make him worry less."

"Whatever. You're right. It's nothing serious, anyway, I agree. Too early for that. It's just a bit of fun." Hearing his words repeated back at him in that flat tone made Taylor feel like a heel. He also didn't like the fact that Draven thought "fun" was the key word for their budding relationship either.

"Draven, I…"

"I had another reason for coming around to see you." Draven ignored him and moved over to the couch and sat down, placing the folder on the scarred wooden table in between the chairs. "I wondered if you could help me with a case I'm working on." He raised that sardonic eyebrow at Taylor's sudden intake of breath.

"What? You thought I wouldn't be able to get past my own inhibitions about what you do and see if there's any truth in what you say you do?"

"Well, yeah, it's a bit surprising." Taylor shuffled forward, suddenly conscious he was in old sweatpants and a grubby tee shirt while Draven was immaculate in a green polo shirt which showed off muscled, blond-haired arms and an impressive set of pectoral muscles. His trendy black jeans looked as if they'd been poured onto him.

Way to impress a man, Taylor, looking like some of hippy guy in a coffee-stained tee.

He slumped next to Draven and ran a hand through the tangled curls of his hair. Draven's eyes followed that movement closely and there was a sudden longing in his eyes that was hard to ignore. Then his face settled back into the blank mask again.

"I'm a businessman. I'll use any tools I need to get what I want and finish the job."

Taylor wasn't sure he liked being called a "tool." He'd been called it in other situations where it had a different meaning but somehow, this dispassionate assessment of what he did seemed worse.

"You do know I'm not something you can just pull out of a fucking cupboard and turn on, don't you?" he said acerbically. "That's not the way this works. I don't even know if I can connect with anything without something emotional binding me to them."

Draven's grey eyes assessed him thoughtfully. "You are emotionally involved," he said. He picked up the folder and waved it. "This is about Drew."

Taylor's heart stopped then stuttered to a slow start again. "Drew?" he whispered. "What about him?"

"I told you I thought someone was blackmailing him about his affairs with men and that was what drove him to kill himself. Now I know that was the case after reviewing the police file. I think he was protecting his family. And I know about protecting family and what you'll do to make sure they survive in this world." Draven's voice was steely. "Now are you going to help me, or not?"

Taylor's first question came out of his mouth without him even realising it. "What do you mean, protecting family? Are yours in danger? Is that where you were tonight?" He leaned forward in concern and hope that perhaps he'd finally get some answers about Draven's secrecy. He laid a hand on Draven's leg, feeling the man tense.

"I don't think that's anything I want to get into with someone who sees me as 'just a bit of fun'," Draven remarked silkily. "Let's just focus on this, shall we?"

He opened the folder and Taylor saw various documents and photographs spill out. He was still stung by Draven's last remark but he had a feeling this wasn't the time to pursue it. He'd try and explain more about what he meant later, when Draven didn't have such a bug up his arse.

"There aren't any pictures of Drew in there are there?" he muttered. "You know, after he killed himself." He definitely wasn't up to seeing one of his lover's heads blown apart at the seams. He really didn't want to pass out again or be sick or anything else around this prickly man.

Draven nodded. "There are, but they're in a separate envelope and you don't need to see them. I'm not that cruel." He indicated to a white A4 envelope splayed across the table. "The thing I really wanted to show you was this."

He handed over a white piece of notepaper with a scrawl on it, a scrawl that Taylor was achingly familiar with.

"It's a copy of the suicide note Drew wrote to his wife, Catherine. I wondered if you could read it, see if you can get any sort of vibe out of it, or whatever it is that you get." Taylor hesitated, not wanting to take the paper. He was scared of what he might see and experience. Draven saw his reluctance.

"It's all right if you don't want to do this," he said evenly. "I'd understand. I've seen what happens to you when you do your thing. I don't want you hurt."

Taylor drew a deep breath. "It's fine. I can do this." He reached out and took the paper from Draven. Almost immediately he felt a sense of suffocation, of grief and emotions that threatened to overwhelm his senses. His vision blurred, his heart sped up and his skin felt clammy. He shook his head, trying to get rid of the sensations invading his body. Through a dim haze, he heard Draven calling his name in panic.

Flashes of light and dark went through his head, blurs of scenes as if they were something out a film, sped up and indistinct, fragments of events that only lasted seconds and made Taylor sick to his stomach with anguish. He heard a man sobbing, felt the warmth of tears down his face, tasted the salt in his mouth and felt cold metal in his right hand. In his vision, he saw a dark-haired woman moving over to Drew, her hands outreached toward him. She seemed familiar. Taylor was falling, falling into an abyss of despair and sorrow and as the cold metal touched the side of his head, the woman screamed.

"Drew, oh God, no. Drew!"

The world went dark.

*****

Once again Draven sat with Taylor's jerking body in his arms, holding the man with all the care he could summon as he passed through whatever it was he saw; Draven only hoped he would come out unscathed. When he'd asked Taylor to touch the paper, he'd never been prepared for a reaction like this. Taylor had gone white, his lips pinched and bloodless, a low keening noise coming out of his mouth like a soul in torment. His eyes had darkened to an unseeing black, a travesty of their usually warm brown, and his body had shivered and trembled.

Draven had tried to pull him back but could only watch helplessly as Taylor shuddered and mumbled and his hands had fidgeted incessantly, bunching up into his tee shirt, exposing his belly and at one time he'd drawn his fingers down the skin, leaving deep scratch marks and blood in their wake. Draven had managed to pull those restless hands away before he could do any more damage and now he sat, heart pounding with fear and shame at having put Taylor through this.

There was no doubt what he was seeing was real. How the whole psychic thing happened he had no idea, but this? This wasn't the natural order of things. This was outside of that. And Draven was both scared and awed by Taylor's abilities.

All the ire he'd felt on Taylor's careless comment to his friend that Draven wasn't anything serious disappeared for the time being by watching this man in the throes of what looked like great sorrow and discomfort.

He managed to get Taylor to the couch and held him tightly, willing him to relax and murmuring soothing platitudes. It was a good fifteen minutes before Taylor's body calmed down and he fell into a deep sleep. Draven slipped off his shoes, got up carefully, easing his aching back, taking care not to wake the sleeping man, although it looked like he was out for the count. He rummaged in Taylor's bedroom for a blanket then came back and lay down on the opposite side of the couch. He pulled the senseless man between his legs, his back against Draven's stomach, head resting on Draven's chest. Draven covered them with the duvet and closed his eyes wearily.

I seem to be making a habit of this. God help me, but there is something about this man that draws me into his orbit and I am going to get burned.

He was dozing when he heard a door open noisily and he came alert instantly. Taylor was still asleep, and Draven's arm was tingling with pins and needles. The light was switched on and he saw a tall, slim, dark-haired man staring down at him with an expression of wariness.

"Who the fuck are you?" The younger man's voice seemed to awaken something in Taylor and he mumbled and opened his eyes. The dark-haired man in high heels and tiny shorts—Draven had to blink twice just to make sure he wasn't in some horny fantasy dream—rushed over and knelt down beside them. He reached out a slim hand and pushed back the duvet, then glared at Draven before falling over the prostate form of Taylor.

Draven oomphed at the press of both bodies weighing him down.

Taylor grumbled and tried to sit up. "I'm okay, Leslie. Give me some space, you freak."

Draven's balls sprang back to life. He heaved a sigh of relief.

"Freak?" Leslie's voice was indignant. Strangely enough, his voice was deeper than Draven would expect from someone dressed like he was. He'd expected a high-pitched girly tone. "You bastard, you're the damn freak. What did this arsehole make you do?"

"Nothing that I didn't want to," mumbled Taylor as he tried to sit up and blinked the sleep out of his eyes. He frowned at Leslie's arm across his waist. "We're working on a case together." He frowned. "I thought you were staying out tonight?"

Leslie's shrugged slim shoulders. "Didn't work out." His eyes narrowed. "So this is Draven...the investigator guy you're fucking?"

"Yes, that would be me." Draven drawled, trying to keep some semblance of dignity even as he was trapped beneath two warm male bodies. In another situation that would have been just the kind of setup he might have appreciated. "Perhaps you can both bloody get off me so I take a pee? My bladder is bursting." He'd been putting it off long enough trying not to wake Taylor up.

Leslie huffed but backed off, allowing Taylor to scramble to his feet. He still looked a little shell-shocked but had more colour than when Draven had technically put him to bed.

"You stayed with me again." His voice was soft, wondering.

Draven grimaced as his bladder threatened to blow. "Of course I did, you idiot. Now can you show me where the damn bathroom is before I wet myself?"

At a vague wave in the direction of the room on the left of the kitchen, Draven hastily made his way to the small toilet and locked the door. He gave a huge gasp of pleasure as his bladder voided itself. Five minutes later he was back in the lounge where Taylor stood, back to him, facing the window and Leslie sat perched on the table, shoes off, rubbing his feet.

Draven cleared his throat and the two men turned to look at him. Taylor's eyes were dulled, dark circles under them but Draven thought he had never looked sexier being so vulnerable. He wanted to wrap this man in a cocoon and never let him go.

"Taylor, are you up to talking about it or should I wait for tomorrow? I know you saw something but I don't want to push you." The last thing in the world Draven wanted was to leave. He wanted to find out from Taylor what had happened, perhaps even get to explore his comment about this being just "fun." It rankled still that that was perhaps how Taylor saw this whole thing.

Leslie glared at him. "Of course it can wait. The man is obviously distressed."

"Leslie." Taylor's voice was firm. "Draven is staying and we're going to my room so we can talk about what I saw. This is important and I need to remember it now while it's still fresh." He bent down and kissed Leslie on his red-streaked black hair. Leslie grunted but reached up and touched Taylor's cheek as if comforting himself.

"You yell if you need me." He cast a suspicious look at Draven. "Don't let *him* wear you out."

Taylor seemed to choke back a laugh. "I promise I won't. Well, he can wear me out only in the ways that matter, anyway." He reached out a hand to Draven as he picked up his duvet. "Come on. We can chat in my room. I have a lot to tell you."

Draven just had time to snatch up the folder and contents before he was pulled along to the bedroom. He followed Taylor in as he closed the door and then found himself the recipient of a mind-blowing, toe-curling kiss as Taylor grabbed his shirt, ground his lips against his and proceeded to mine the inside of his mouth.

The folder dropped to the floor and Draven didn't give a fuck. He'd never been so thoroughly excavated. As a hungry, wet tongue entwined with his and small gasps of breath escaped both of their mouths, Draven felt a sense of belonging. Of ownership and being owned. It was the strangest sensation to realise that fact as warm hands crept into his shirt and caressed skin that was set on fire. Taylor pushed him backward onto the bed, straddling him, dark curls falling down across his face, eyes shining with feverish intensity and mouth red and swollen from kisses.

"Thank you for staying with me," he breathed against Draven's ear as he trailed a hot tongue down skin that suddenly felt too tight for his body. Draven tingled with every sense he had. "I'm sorry this relationship seems to always end in me passing out and you having to rescue me."

"Relationship?" Draven gasped as hands unbuckled his trousers and Taylor's palm bore down on the erection that was about to erupt from his pants. "I thought you said this was only a bit of fun." He uttered a deep groan as warm lips mouthed his highly sensitive cock through the black briefs he wore. His hands clenched into Taylor's hair.

"I lied. I told you, I just want them to stop pestering me about things and thinking I can't take care of myself. I'm a big boy. I know what I want. And fuck, I want you so badly. In me. Now. The talk can wait."

Those words drilled directly down into Draven's dick. His balls were tucked tight in his groin and he shuddered.

"Christ, Taylor. I am going to come right now if you keep saying things like that to me." He lifted his hips as Taylor tugged on his trousers and shuffled back to pull them down with his briefs. He licked his lips, his eyes feasting on Draven, naked from the waist down, the biggest erection Draven thought he'd ever had begging for attention. Thick, swollen, leaking and rosy and Draven was very proud of it.

Taylor reached up and pulled off his shirt in one sexy move, revealing a torso that was almost hairless, just a faint dark treasure trail down to the a groin that definitely was ready for action from the tenting of the sweatpants.

Draven's eyes followed him as he stood up above him, on the bed, and slid his pants down his legs. Taylor stepped out of them and gave them a careless kick with his foot. The pants landed in a puddle on the floor. Draven lost his breath at the sight of so much male magnificence standing above him, that beautiful purple cock that thrust proudly from wiry black curls. Heavy balls hung below his groin, and Taylor gave a wicked grin and shimmied his hips, causing both cock and balls to move decadently. Draven's mouth watered at the sight.

He reached over and gripped Taylor, pulling him forward. Taylor gave a breathy sigh and fell to his knees. All that beauty and sexiness got closer and Draven wanted to taste it so badly. He shuffled up the bed backward, toward the wall, and pulled Taylor's hips toward him. Taylor's pupils were blown, his chest heaving, lips pouty and wet and Draven leaned forward and engulfed that beautiful prick in his mouth, wrapping his tongue around it, licking and sucking and hearing Taylor's grunts and moans as he paid undivided attention to that swollen part of him that needed release. Draven loved feasting on cock, loved the slickness and heat in his mouth, the taste of it, the burn at the back of his throat when he deep throated.

Taylor moaned in displeasure when Draven released him.

"God, don't stop. Please don't stop." His voice was ragged, his body almost vibrating with need.

Draven smiled wolfishly. "Don't worry. I have no intention of stopping. Just needed some air before I tell you to fuck my mouth."

Taylor gasped, eyes widening and Draven pulled him even closer. "Let me see you lose it. Then you can ride me, because, honey, I think that would be the most beautiful sight in the world. You riding my cock."

Taylor groaned and rammed his dick into Draven's mouth. Draven held Taylor's eyes as it disappeared deep inside his willing lips. Taylor's eyes were mirrors of hazy ecstasy as he pumped in and out of Draven's needy mouth, his movements getting more erratic as he gasped and moaned his way to orgasm. Draven alternated between closing his eyes to appreciate what he had in his mouth to opening them to see Taylor above him, looking down with those dark eyes and wet lips. For a minute, Draven didn't think he'd make it long enough to have that ride he was promised. He gripped the base of his cock with one hand, willing it not to explode before he was inside Taylor.

His other hand slid between Taylor's firm cheeks, as he sought the opening he wanted. Taylor moaned as Draven slid a finger inside, slick with his own fluids. He had the lube ready but for now, he thought this was all that was needed to open Taylor up.

"Oh, God, that's it, just fuck me with your fingers," Taylor whimpered. "So damn good."

It took a while but finally there was a rhythm, Taylor pushing into his mouth while Draven fucked his arse as he pushed away and out. It wasn't perfect but it didn't matter. Draven now had three fingers in Taylor's hole as he impaled himself with each thrust backward.

Taylor gave a grunt, then a loud cry and his cock swelled in Draven's mouth as warm come flooded his tongue, slid down his throat and Taylor pressed hands against the wall for support as he slowly stopped thrusting. For a while, there was only the sound of Taylor panting, and Draven's lip smacking as he relished Taylor's essence. Draven was quite content to lie there, one hand on Taylor's hips, the other still tightly gripping his engorged cock.

Taylor leaned down and kissed him, mouth still hungry and Draven knew the best was still to come.

"Get yourself ready for me," he whispered. "I want to see you do it."

Taylor nodded and reached over him. There was the sound of a drawer opening, some activity and then Draven watched while Taylor opened the lube and spread it on his fingers. Then he nearly came as Taylor reached around himself and with a wicked smile, he began to prep his hole for Draven.

"I don't think I need much," he murmured. "You seem to have made quite a good job of doing it while I was otherwise engaged."

He threw the tube down and opened the condom, rolling it out on Draven's cock, grinning as his fingers slyly caressed the tip and the sides as he did so.

"Taylor, can it," Draven growled, trying hard to keep himself from flying into orbit. "Just get on."

"Say please," Taylor whispered as he positioned himself above Draven with a smirk.

"Please, baby."

Taylor moaned softly as he lowered himself down and when Draven found his needy cock enmeshed in the tight, hot embrace of Taylor's body, he wanted to howl like a wolf. The sight of this beautiful, coffee-coloured man with the wild eyes and even wilder hair riding him like a mustang was enough to make him wonder how he'd ever survived without it. The feeling of his cock being slickly and expertly manipulated inside Taylor and the soft, panting of the man driving him out of his mind were like nirvana. He never wanted it to end.

Emotions swelled in his chest as Taylor smiled down at him, already semi-hard again and Draven reached over and gripped Taylor's cock as he performed the most graceful and erotic ballet on Draven that he'd ever experienced.

Time was not something to be measured now, but rather luxuriated in, embraced and absorbed like the treasure it was, each minute special, unique and each essence and smell something to be revelled in. Draven came inside Taylor with an explosion of desire, affection and passion, his body a slave to the man who held it in his thrall and who was slowly doing the same to his heart.

Taylor climaxed again too, hot streams of semen streaming across Draven's stomach and chest as finally, the performance was over and the actors took their bows off each other.

They lay together afterwards, limbs entwined, both wet and sweaty with the smell of sex. Taylor's hands gently strayed across Draven's chest, fingers gentle and soothing. He felt as if he'd been dipped in a vat of thick honey, his arms and legs barely moving and the taste in his mouth of both Taylor and his kisses sweet and sticky.

"Do you believe me when I told you I don't just see you as a bit of fun?" Taylor nibbled at Draven's nipple, causing him to shiver in delight.

"So wasn't what we did here tonight fun then?" Draven smiled as Taylor huffed in exasperation.

"You know what I mean. Don't be bloody obtuse."

"Big word, small fry," Draven chuckled as Taylor pinched the skin at his waist. "Ouch. Yes, I think I believe you. I still can't believe we've gone from disliking each other to having mad passionate sex nearly every night."

"Believe it," Taylor whispered as his hands drifted lower toward Draven's groin. "And from the feel of it, you're ready to go again…"

Draven shook his head and stayed Taylor's wandering hands. Much as he wanted to make love again, he wanted to hear about Taylor's visions more.

"Oh no, you don't. We said we were going to talk and then you ravaged me. So now we get to have that conversation."

Taylor pouted and Draven was smitten all over again. The man was adorable.

"Fine." He sat up, covers falling from his waist, and sat cross-legged on the bed, splendid in his nakedness. He was so relaxed about his body. Draven sat up, making sure his nether regions were hidden from Taylor's prying eyes and squinted as Taylor leaned over to light a cigarette taken from a pack in the bedside drawer.

Draven sighed heavily. "So stereotypical. Smoking after sex? Really?"

Taylor shrugged as he took a deep drag and made sure to blow the smoke away from Draven. "So sue me. If I have to tell this damn story, I need a cigarette." He narrowed his eyes. "But this is an 'I'll tell you mine, you tell me yours' situation. Afterward, I want to hear about your family and what makes you want to protect them."

He raised an eyebrow as Draven visibly squirmed at that statement. "There's no negotiation. Either you let me into your private life just a little…hell, you know enough about mine…or I stay *schtum* about what I saw in my vision."

Draven could see Taylor wouldn't be dissuaded. And it would be good to share something about Jude with someone who wasn't a doctor, a nurse or a pro-lifer.

"Agreed. You first."

The tip of the cigarette glowed red in the light of the room as Taylor took a drag. "I felt him in that room he died in. Drew was sitting at the desk. He was crying."

Draven felt a chill. The suicide note had shown traces of salt and other chemicals associated with tears but that was something Taylor wouldn't have known. However it was a pretty reasonable assumption to make. The man *had* killed himself for God's sake.

"He was writing the note and the tears were falling on it. He had to keep wiping them away so he could keep writing. It's why there were smudges in the ink. I noticed it when I read the note. Some parts were blurred." Taylor's voice was distant. Draven thought it was hard to believe that only half an hour ago they'd been in the throes of sexual passion. "It isn't all that clear; I've filled in some of the gaps myself. But they feel right. For whatever reason, I saw more than I usually do this time. It was more…like a jerky black-and-white film, with missing scenes. That hasn't happened before."

He took a deep breath. "He had a note with him, some typewritten thing. I couldn't see it, but he kept saying, 'Why would anyone do this? Who cares if I'm seeing men that they would do this to me?' He wrote the note, saying he was sorry, but it was better this way than destroying his family any more. Then he burnt the other note in the dustbin. He took the gun out of the drawer. He kept in the right-hand side. He was right handed, so I guess that made sense."

Taylor went quiet and Draven thought he'd gone to sleep or into one of his fugues. He leaned forward to check and started when Taylor started speaking again. "He toyed with the gun a while, looking at it, smelling it, as if he wanted to remember what it felt like. He was so unhappy, so tormented. Whatever it was, he felt the only way out was dying. I can't imagine how desperate he must have been."

Draven leaned forward and touched a hand to Taylor's cheek.

Taylor's voice was taut. "He said goodbye to everyone he loved, then he just raised the gun and shot himself." Taylor shivered, a full-body shudder, and Draven pulled him into his arms.

Taylor's voice was muffled as he pressed his face into Draven's shoulder. "But someone was with him just before he pulled the trigger. A woman."

Draven went still. "There was no one with him when he died, according to the family. He was alone. His wife says she got home a little while later and found the body."

Taylor sat up. "There was someone there, I saw and heard her. She shouted out 'No, Drew, no' just as he shot himself. She sounded …panicked, so damned shocked. Then everything went black. I think it was his wife, but I only saw the back of her."

Draven sat back, feeling bone tired. "You didn't get a chance to read the note before you went all *Red Lights* on me. He basically said that he'd brought shame upon his family by being with men and he didn't want them to suffer. So he thought the best thing was to take himself out of the equation."

"He killed himself because someone found about his bisexuality?" Taylor's hands waved in the air. "That's no damn reason; he could have talked about to his wife, his family, not killed himself."

"There was more." Draven knew this was inevitable but he still dreaded the fallout it would cause with Taylor. "Someone had videos of him fucking other men. Not just that, there was other stuff as well, more kinky shit. It was all over the internet. They threatened to make it public if he didn't pay up. It all seemed to take place at some club called Dive Bomb out in Sussex somewhere."

Taylor's body went still. "He asked me to go there with him once," he said quietly. "I looked it up and didn't quite fancy the whole scene. A little much for me. I declined. Just as well or I'd be all over the internet too, wouldn't I?" He giggled slightly hysterically and Draven held him tighter. "I have to ask, was there anything you saw where he was fucking me or the other way around?"

Draven kissed Taylor's raven curls. "No. Don't you think I would have told you that fact first? There was nothing involving you. I'm glad you didn't go to that BDSM club though. You'd definitely be in the film, the latest porn star to hit the news. And I only want you to be my porn star. No one else's."

They were both silent, thinking about the cruelty of someone driving a decent man to kill himself. Draven had a story to finish.

"So he told his family about it all, the whole truth and then shot himself. He decided it was the only way for his family to move on. He knew it might go public afterward anyway; they might do it out of spite for not giving over the money. He thought with him dead the scandal would die a quicker death. He was CEO of a huge multinational company after all, worth millions. He even left instructions in his will for a new CEO and Management Board to run the company in his absence."

"And now we have a mystery on our hands," Taylor said softly. "And I only hope I'm going to be able to help you figure it out. This gift I have…it's not an exact science, you know, but it's all we seem to have."

Draven ran fingers through soft hair, and smiled as he placed a kiss on the top of Taylor's head.

"You're amazing at this stuff. No one who has seen what you can do could doubt you know, least of all me. I was an arsehole, I admit it. I didn't believe in you, but now I do."

Taylor grimaced. "You don't have to flatter me for sex. I'll do you for free." But he shot a quick smile at Draven as he swung his legs out of bed. "I need to take a piss. Don't go far."

He disappeared out of the bedroom and appeared back a few minutes later. He climbed into bed and Draven grumbled.

"Christ, you're frozen. Come here, let me warm you up."

They snuggled back up under the duvet and Draven was half asleep when Taylor spoke sleepily.

"So this woman I saw. Do you think it was the wife?"

Draven opened a groggy eye. "I dunno. Maybe the wife was lying. Would you recognise the voice if you heard it? Or her appearance from the back?"

"I think so." Taylor's voice was uncertain. "Definitely the voice anyway."

"Well, maybe we'll take a trip to Drew's house. Pay our respects to the family. We might get lucky and you might recognise who she is." He was aware of Taylor's body stiffening beside him.

"I don't want to see them. I have no place there," he muttered stubbornly.

Draven sighed. "It's for Drew, Taylor. We're trying to solve a murder, because to me that's what this is. Someone drove him to kill himself and in my book that's murder."

Taylor huffed quietly. "You sound like that guy in *Hart to Hart*. The factotum guy who travels around with them." He put on a terrible accent. "I take care of both of them…which ain't easy; 'cause when they met it was murder." He pronounced it *moi-der* like the man in the TV show, and Draven groaned theatrically. He noticed Taylor didn't object to going anymore though. He must have really liked Drew.

"God, not only are you reminding me of bad American TV shows, you really mangled that accent. Go to sleep, Tay. I'll see about getting us in to see the family in the morning. Then if you're a good boy to me," he made the words as suggestive as he could, "I'll take you to an early dinner."

Taylor cuddled up against him with a chuckle and Draven felt the prod of a semi-hard erection in his back.

"'Kay. Sleep tight. If you fancy taking advantage me in the middle of the night, just wake me up."

Draven smiled in the darkness. "I'll bear that in mind. G'night."

He lay for a while listening to Taylor fall asleep and the sound of his steady breathing. He was relieved that Taylor seemed to have forgotten all about Draven spilling his guts out about his throwaway family comment.

Perhaps for the time being, that was the better option. The more Draven told people about Jude, the more likelihood they'd have an opinion on what he should be doing. Just like Doctor Frederick at the hospital. For a while longer, Jude was his and no one else's. The decision he needed to make was buried deep inside him and for the moment, he didn't want it letting out to take root and bear fruit.

Chapter 8

The following morning, Taylor woke around eight and watched Draven sleep. His dark blond hair was mussed, his lips twitching in some dream, and his hands curled into the duvet as if in the throes of a pleasurable dream. Hands that had caressed Taylor, driven him crazy with want and finally ended up releasing him from the pent-up sexual frustration he'd had.

The memory of their rather energetic and raunchy love-making session echoed in Taylor's mind, his body still sore from being so fully taken and possessed. He reached out a hand and touched Draven's cheek and was rewarded by the glint of sleepy grey eyes as Draven awoke. For a moment both men stared at each other, dark chocolate meeting stormy seas and for a moment, the world ceased. It was as if somewhere, somehow, they were the only two people on earth.

Then the spell was broken by a loud knock at the door.

"Taylor. Get your debauched arse out of bed. There's a phone call for you." Leslie's voice reverberated through the door and Draven grinned, his face mischievous.

"He's got your number, Mr. Debauched. I still have a beautiful memory of you riding my cock as if I were a thoroughbred stallion." He sat up in bed, the duvet falling to his waist and revealing a semi hard-on in the process.

Taylor flushed as he got out of bed. "Yes, well, I was a little horny last night." He pulled on a pair of shorts, not missing Draven's interested glance at the fact they were rather tight and clingy and showed everything off to best advantage.

"Taylor, are you in there? The person said he'd call back in five minutes. Get off that man and get dressed." Leslie's voice was amused with a hint of impatience and Draven chuckled.

"He sounds like a real peach," he remarked as he swung his leg out of bed and padded naked to the door. "Maybe I should surprise him."

Before Taylor could object, Draven had opened the door and stood there revealed in all his glory to a wide-eyed Leslie, who looked as if he had been about to knock. He was dressed in plum-coloured silk pyjamas that clung to his slim frame.

"You were looking for Taylor?" Draven drawled lazily, his cock bobbing as he scratched his balls.

Leslie smiled widely and looked pointedly down at Draven's groin. "I don't blame him for being distracted with *that* at his beck and call," he said silkily. "I can see why he likes you so much." His eyebrows rose in a question. "Is there room for one more when you guys play next?"

Taylor sniggered, both at Draven's look at Leslie's calm reaction to him being naked and at the look of discomfort that crossed his face at the question. Taylor knew Leslie was joking—he had a specific aversion to threesomes or more and for Leslie, a free-minded spirit, he was considered quite a prude on the subject. Taylor had often been on the receiving side of Leslie's lectures about love making being between two people and another person simply making things complicated. Taylor himself had no such aversion and had been a willing participant in such situations before. He waited now to see what Draven would say.

Draven cast a quick glance at Taylor, who kept his face blank. "Uhm, I'm not sure that's a good idea," he said carefully, with another glance at Taylor. "I mean, I'd really prefer to have Tay to myself, nothing against you, but I think, you know, sex is between two people."

Leslie gave a loud squeal of pleasure and wrapped arms around Draven's neck. His cock was pressed against cool silk and it twitched at the friction of being accosted by what seemed like an octopus.

"Good for you, Tay. You found another believer." He pulled away and then licked his lips lasciviously. "And what a believer he is. Hung like a fucking rhinoceros."

Taylor laughed as he pulled Draven into the bedroom. "I'm pretty pleased too. Now you'd better get dressed," he motioned at Draven then turned to Leslie. "Any idea who it was on the phone?"

Leslie shrugged. "He was from work, wondering whether you were going on in today. Chris something or the other."

Taylor frowned. "I'm on a few days' leave this week, he should know that. I'll give work a call in a minute, remind them I've got the time off. Draven and I have some plans today."

Leslie grinned. "Do they involve you two locking yourselves in the bedroom and rutting like rabbits?"

Taylor shook his head, smiling at that thought because, honestly, he liked the sound of that. "No, you idiot. We have to go visit someone for the case Draven's working on." He waved at Leslie. "Now be gone with you so we can get dressed. I think you've seen enough of my guy for one day."

He smiled politely at his friend, pulled Draven back into the room and closed the door firmly. There was a snort of laughter from the other side.

"You two are so going back to bed and doing the bunny thing. I just know it!"

Draven raised an eyebrow as he stood there, still magnificently nude. "Is he right?"

Taylor snickered. "Much as I fancy that idea, no." He opened the scratched and pitted door of his small wardrobe and took out a threadbare but clean towel. "We're going to shower and go and do this thing with Drew's family." He handed the towel to Draven who wrapped it around his waist. It covered his private bits but left little to the imagination. As Draven had already been revealed in all his glory, Taylor didn't think he'd mind a little more "flasher" activity. "The bathroom is at the end of the hall. Take a shower and I'll be in after you. Then we can get this whole visit out of the way."

Draven reached out a hand and caressed Taylor's jawline gently. "Are you okay with this? You're not going to have another meltdown, are you? Because I don't think I want to see you lose it again."

Taylor's eyes softened. "I'll be fine. It's just listening to her voice and seeing if she's the same woman as in my dream, right? As long as I don't touch anything while I'm there, it'll be okay. That seems to be when these things spark it off."

Draven opened the door and peered out into the corridor, looking for the all clear. "Feel free to join me in the shower if you like," he said mischievously as he padded barefoot down the hallway.

Taylor chuckled. "Not likely. The shower barely fits one person, let alone two doing the vertical hump. Maybe we can try that out at your place."

"I heard that!" came a sing-song voice from Leslie's bedroom. "Dirty bastards, the two of you." His comment was followed by a loud snigger and Taylor rolled his eyes. He loved his friend but he was like a damn jackdaw, all cheeky, bright-eyed and inquisitive.

He grabbed another towel and followed Draven down into the bathroom. He might not be able to fit into the shower, but there was nothing to stop him lusting after the man while he was naked with water running down his body.

*****

An hour later they were in Draven's car, on their way to Drew's home on Crooked Mile in Waltham Abbey. Draven said he'd been there a couple of times before when he worked with Drew on the ultra-secretive case he'd had when he'd helped him with his business espionage issue. Taylor was dying to hear that story but Draven was very close-mouthed about it. Like he was about a *lot* of things about himself, Taylor had to admit. Thinking about that, he shot a glance at Draven as he drove. He wanted to ask about his ultimatum on "I'll tell you mine, you tell me yours" but wasn't sure whether he wanted to chance any fallout when the man was driving.

Draven turned and smiled at him. "You okay there? Is my driving up to scratch?" His voice was teasing.

Taylor grinned. "Yeah. I don't think I'll be puking my guts out anytime soon."

Capable fingers threaded the wheel as Draven manoeuvred his way around a large farm trailer.

He seems in a really good mood. I guess now is as good a time as any to ask.

"Draven, I still didn't get my wish to find out what it is that makes you need to protect your family. You promised me the story and I'm holding you to it."

He groaned inwardly as Draven's fingers clenched on the wheel and hastened to qualify his statement. "I mean, I don't want to pry but I'd like to share. You know stuff about me that I've never told anyone before. Hell, you've watched me pass out a few times and be sick in a street bin. You've definitely seen me at my worst."

The silence echoed in the car and finally Draven turned and glanced at him. There was a slight frown on his face coupled with a look of sorrow in his eyes. Then his gaze shifted back to the front.

"It's nothing dramatic, Taylor. Just a family tragedy that means I have a decision to make in the near future. One I really don't want to make." He scowled and Taylor laid a hand on his leg.

"Then tell me about it and maybe I can help."

Draven frowned darkly. "It's not something you can help with. Why all the curiosity about my situation, anyway?"

Taylor sighed heavily. Draven's mood seemed to have changed within seconds, going from the playful demeanour of before to a moody individual hell-bent on keeping secrets.

"Fine, don't worry about it. It'll keep, I guess, until you're willing to tell me. Far be it from me to force anything out of you."

He stared forward, fingers tapping nervously on his jeans-clad leg. They drove in silence, the air in the car thick with tension. The busy road ahead looked like a ribbon of motorcars, exhaust pipes belching plumes of smoke, trucks whizzing past with no care as to the speed limit and endless paths of concrete and tarmac in view.

Finally Draven sighed and reached out and stayed his hand. "Three years ago my parents were killed in a car accident."

Taylor swallowed. "I'm sorry, Draven. That must have been really tough to get through." He didn't really know what else to say. There was a deep quiet in the car before Draven spoke again.

"My little brother Jude was in the car with them. He survived." He gave a sharp laugh with no discernible trace of amusement that Taylor could hear. "If you can call it that. He's been in a coma ever since they pulled him out of the wreck. He was just heading for his sixteenth birthday."

His voice was flat, tired and dispirited. Taylor had heard men's voices that sounded like that before. Like the day Bobby Meredith's father found out his son would never be coming home. It chilled Taylor, made him remember all the voices he'd heard in his head and the sad sounds of their dying. He shivered, a full-body tremor that shook him to his core.

"Where is he?" he asked quietly. "In a hospital somewhere? Is that where you go when you turn your phone off?"

Draven was still, eyes focused on the country road ahead. They'd left the main road behind and were meandering down country lanes filled with picturesque houses and chocolate-box fields and greens. Far ahead in front, Taylor saw the back of what looked like a Bentley from the looks of the badge. This area was obviously fairly affluent.

"He's in the Royal." Draven finally answered. "And yes, I spend a fair amount of time there with him."

"How bad is he?" Taylor shifted in his seat and pressed down on Draven's leg, hoping the touch brought comfort. Draven overtook the Bentley rather adroitly and Taylor held his breath. From the driver-side window, a silver-haired man glared at them as they whizzed past smoothly.

"He's not good. Very low on the coma scale to the point of being…" Draven's voice caught. "Let's just say every time I go in there it's possible it might be the last time I see him."

Taylor pulled in a breath in horror. "That really sucks." He couldn't imagine being faced with such a terrible burden. Something niggled in the back of his brain, that little second sense that told him perhaps he'd felt something about Draven's pain already; that somehow he'd known. Draven's next growled words made him forget that train of thought.

"It's a nightmare, a cosmic fucking joke that someone like Jude could be like he was…he was always so lively and fun and now…" His broad shoulders shrugged. "I live in hope that one day things will get better, but it's getting to the stage where I can't really be positive about it anymore." His face tightened. "The worse thing about it is not knowing if he's in pain, if there's anything of my little brother still living inside that body. It rips my heart out every time I see him."

"I'd like to meet him," Taylor murmured. "Maybe one day you'll take me there to visit."

Draven didn't answer, but started to slow the car down. "This is it," he muttered. "Drew's place. Fancy isn't it?"

Taylor filed away the fact that he hadn't agreed to take him to see his brother, but let it go. There was time enough to pursue it later. At least he knew a little more about where Draven went at nights when he didn't answer his phone. He felt sick at what Draven was going through and even worse for the young man in the hospital bed with what seemed like little chance of recovery. Taylor's heart ached for them both but especially for his lover being left to pick up the pieces.

Taylor just wished Draven would let him help.

His sympathy at Draven's plight was temporarily forgotten as he saw the house and felt a spark of surprise at its opulence. It could be seen set back from the road, a huge mansion of pale grey cobblestone set in what looked like a national park, with a sweeping driveway up which they now drove, through opened wrought-iron metal gates. The front door stood above a set above of regal steps, about twenty feet in width, with a stone balustrade either side.

Draven pulled up, turned off the engine and undid his seat belt.

"Wow," Taylor exclaimed softly. "That is something. Makes my place look like a hovel." He climbed out of the car and followed Draven, who was already striding toward the steps. Draven turned to look behind him, one eyebrow raised.

"Come on then. Let's see who's at home. I did call earlier to make sure Catherine was in today. I didn't tell her to expect us. I like the element of surprise."

"So do I," Taylor remarked drily as he followed him up the stairs. "So don't think I've forgotten about your story and meeting your brother. I'll make sure to follow that up sometime."

Draven turned back and stared at him with a strange look then smiled slightly and dipped his head in acknowledgement. He rang the bell and from inside, a there was a loud chiming sound. Taylor's stomach plunged to his feet and he willed the sick feeling he had in his gut away.

There is no fucking way on this earth that you are going to pass out in front of him again. So suck it the fuck up you big baby and fight it.

There was no doubt that some of the emotions he'd originally felt around Drew's death were present in his head, simmering bubbles of agitation and grief. He and Drew might have been occasional lovers but there was no doubt that Taylor had been very fond of him. He sometimes caught Draven watching him carefully when he talked about him. Taylor could see the curiosity in his eyes, the question there as to whether Taylor had felt more for Drew beyond being a fuck buddy. Well, the answer was yes, but it had been more of a fondness for another human being and not the overwhelming passion Taylor seemed to have for the man currently standing next to him.

There was no point in taunting himself with what-ifs, Taylor thought sadly. Perhaps in another life, he and Drew might have meant more to each other. But now they'd never know.

He took his hands out of his pockets to run fingers through his hair and just as quickly shoved them back in, not wanting to chance a reaction to the emotions running through the house, or accidentally touch anything.

Maybe I need to get myself a pair of gloves. A sexy pair of leather ones that I can tease Draven's dick with.

He swallowed a chuckle at that thought even as his dick stirred in his pants. Draven frowned and rang the bell again. Then he knocked loudly using the brass handle fixed to the door. He stepped back and surveyed the surroundings, his keen slate eyes narrowing.

"I know someone's home. I saw them in one of the upstairs rooms when we got out of the car."

Taylor was impressed. "Wow. You can take the investigator out of the city but you can't take the investigator out of the man. Are you always so observant?"

Draven grinned wolfishly. "I had noticed that slight boner in your pants. What the hell were you thinking about to put that there?"

Taylor's mouth fell open. "You…what? Honestly?" He took a quick look down at his groin. Yes, he wasn't particularly soft but he didn't think anyone would have noticed his semi hard-on.

Draven snorted softly in laughter. "I tend to notice everything about you, Taylor. I really think…"

What Draven thought was cut off as the door opened and a man's voice said, "Yes? Can I help you?"

Taylor thought he'd stepped out into the pages of a detective novel written by Agatha Christie, one of his favourite authors. It was the man he'd seen at the funeral. He looked like the archetypical butler, grey hair, regal bearing, dressed in a white shirt and a black suit. His rather bushy eyebrows were raised, and he had a rather querulous expression on his face.

Draven stepped forward. "My name is Draven Samuels and I was a friend of Drew's. This is my friend, Taylor Abelard. He also knew Drew. We're here to pay our respects to Catherine and see how she is. I did call ahead and told someone I'd be stopping by and to expect us."

Taylor opened his mouth to say something about that outright lie then shut it. A sneaking pride suffused his body at the effortless way his lover lied so smoothly and confidently. Then he thought about possibly being on the receiving end of Draven's lying mastery one day and his admiration turned to apprehension.

The man at the door sighed heavily. "Well, please do come in. No one told me we were expecting visitors. Catherine's been a bit distraught today and my daughter isn't very good at dealing with things."

Draven nodded. "I'm sorry. Would you prefer we came back another time then?"

God, Draven is so charming, even when he's suggesting something he doesn't really want to do.

Not the butler, Catherine's father. He shook his head. "No, don't worry. To be honest, I'd be glad of the male company. Being surrounded by a bunch of hysterical females gives me somewhat of a headache. My wife and daughter have been a bit of a trial." He beckoned to Draven to enter. Taylor followed close behind, feeling empathy for Catherine at the same time he felt the start of dislike for the man currently showing them in.

The woman lost a husband, for God's sake. The man could have a little bit of patience, surely?

From the flaring of Draven's nostrils, Taylor thought he felt the same way. He fidgeted, trying to suppress the emotions that coated him like soft ash, settling on his skin and making him itch. To distract himself, he stared around the palatial entrance hall, with marbled floors, fancy, ornate light fittings and a long flight of stairs that seemed to lead up to the next level. It was plush, luxurious and so unlike the Drew he'd known that he felt a little gobsmacked. His Drew had been happy to eat takeout from Chinese-labelled containers, lie on the wet spot and listen to music on his iPhone while lolling on the lumpy hotel couch. This all seemed too extravagant for the man and Taylor guessed more of the house décor was to do with Catherine's needs, not Drew's.

"Are you okay?" Draven said quietly. "Not going to weird out on me, are you?"

Taylor shook his head. "As long as I keep my hands in my pockets, I'll be fine. It's a little overwhelming, but I'm managing."

Draven regarded him with a concerned look then turned back as the man at his side extended a hand.

"Jack Threadcourt. As I said, I'm Catherine's dad."

Draven shook his hand. "Glad to meet you, sir. I'm really sorry about Drew. He was a good man."

Jack's face darkened. "I thought he was. Then we found about his other, ahem…preferences. I wouldn't have minded if he'd come clean and told us he was gay and had some rather dubious habits. Instead he chose to cheat on my daughter then killed himself when someone found out. I think that was the coward's way out."

He turned and walked toward one of the rooms off the entrance hall. "Let me see if I can find Catherine. She was sleeping in the lounge while my wife watched over her. If you two gentleman would like to wait in the conservatory, I'll let her know you're here. It's that room over there." He waved a hand in the direction of a sun-drenched room to his right and strode off.

Taylor's knees threatened to give way at that. His old insecurity about him being a slut and pandering to Drew's needs reared to the fore. And yes, Drew might have had other options than pulling the trigger but who knew what was in the mind of a man who had had a deep, dark secret of the kind he had.

Draven moved over to his side, his presence a comfort, and gave Taylor's arm a slight squeeze. "You didn't encourage him and you are not a slut." Draven's whispered words were a balm to Taylor's soul. "So take that panicked look off your face and man up."

Taylor gave him a grateful glance.

How the hell does he do that? Can he read my damn mind? God, how weird would that be, both of us being special.

Draven grasped his elbow and led him over to the waiting room. They both sat down on plush seats made of some very expensive-looking fabric and waited.

*****

Draven watched Taylor closely. He knew the man well enough by now to see the constant fidgeting, the slight frown marking that expressive face, the full lips pressed together as Taylor tried to suppress whatever it was he was feeling. He could see Taylor was uncomfortable being in Drew's house; not just for the emotions he seemed to be picking up, but for the fact that he felt like a thief in the night stealing another man away from his family, even if only for sex and companionship. Not for the first time, Draven wondered exactly how close Drew and Taylor had been. To hear Taylor say it, they'd been occasional fuck buddies, albeit fond of each other and that was it. However, Taylor's reactions seemed to indicate more than that. Draven felt a prickle of jealousy and he quelled it, admonishing himself internally for being jealous of a dead man.

They both started as a loud wail echoed from a room on the other side of the house, somewhere in the bowels of the mansion. It was a cry rent with grief and pain.

"No, Daddy. I can't do this anymore. Tell them to leave, tell them to go. Please." The sound dissolved into heart-rending sobs. Draven shivered when he heard it—even more so when he saw Taylor's reaction to the sound. Taylor went ghostly white, his dark eyes shadowing and his hands incessantly moving in his pockets. The agitated stare levelled at Draven told him everything he needed to know. This must be the woman whose voice Taylor had heard in his vision—Drew's wife, Catherine.

He moved closer to his lover, reaching out to touch an arm that felt like whipcord, taut and immovable. It was as if Taylor was set in granite. Draven felt a sense of unease at the small movements of Taylor's bloodless lips, as if he was chanting a prayer or incanting something to ward off evil spirits. He gripped Taylor's chin firmly, forcing him to look at him.

"That's the woman's voice you heard?" he murmured as Taylor nodded jerkily and then closed his eyes, his face stilling. Draven cursed softly as he recognised all the signs of one of Taylor's classic meltdowns. He expected the man to fall unconscious to the floor at any minute.

"Taylor." He shook him hard; gripping his arm, leaving what he was sure would be bruises. He needed to stop what was happening. "Look at me. Look at me!"

Taylor's eyes opened, revealing panicked dark orbs and Draven leaned into him. "You are going to be fine. Go outside and get some fresh air. I'll finish up here and then our job is done. You hear me? You did it, baby. Now go," He pushed Taylor toward the entrance. "Wait for me outside. I'll be there soon. And for God's sake don't faint and fall down the stairs. Hold onto the rail, you hear me?"

Once again Taylor nodded as ragged breaths forced out of his body. He turned and fled the house, opening the front door and slamming it shut behind him just as Jack Threadcourt made his way toward Draven across the entrance hall. His face was wearied, lips pinched and Draven thought he was seeing yet another man at the end of his tether.

Jack raised his hands apologetically. He stopped and glanced at the front door with a slight frown. "I'm sorry, Mr. Samuels. Catherine's really not up to visitors at the moment. I'm sure you heard that outburst." He sighed. "My wife is sitting with her now, but honestly, I think it would be best if you left and tried another day. Perhaps give it a few days then call ahead again. It will save you wasting your time coming here."

Draven nodded and extended a hand to shake Jack's. "I completely understand, Mr. Threadcourt. It's a terrible situation and I have no desire to make it worse for any of you." He waved at the front door. "Taylor wasn't feeling too well—a little emotional himself, I think—so I sent him out to get some air. I'll definitely call again and see if we can come by. Thank you for trying anyway."

Jack led the way to the door and opened it. Taylor sat on the steps of the house smoking, and Draven felt a surge of relief that he looked better; his colour was back and his eyes weren't as tortured as they had been. As the door opened, he stood up and stared uncertainly at Jack.

"Thank you for letting us in, Mr. Threadcourt," Taylor said softly as he extended his hand. "We appreciate you trying to let us see her and I'm sorry if we upset her."

Jack sighed as he shook the offered hand. "Don't worry. It's been a really tough time for her, and I'm just pleased she has people who care about her."

Draven placed a hand on the small of Taylor's back. He wanted to make sure he didn't have sort of turn and fall down the broad steps. Taylor smiled at him gently.

Draven nodded. "Thank you, sir. I'll be in touch soon."

A few minutes later both of them were seated in the car watching the door at the top of the stairs shut with finality.

Taylor shifted in the seat as he pulled his seat belt on and regarded Draven with a slight look of amusement. "Baby?"

"What?" asked Draven distractedly as he too put his belt on and started the car.

"Back there, in the house. You called me 'baby'."

Draven frowned. "Did I? Oh." There was silence as he pulled off and drove down the winding drive toward the open gates. He felt a little embarrassed. "Shouldn't I have? I mean, it just slipped out. It's okay if you don't want me to call you that, I won't do it again…"

"Draven." Taylor laid a warm hand on his leg and squeezed. "It's fine. Don't get all wiggy about it. I just didn't expect it from you, that's all."

Draven nodded slowly. "Okay. So I'm not in trouble?"

Taylor leaned over and cast a soft kiss on Draven's stubbled cheek. It tingled. "No. I rather liked it actually."

Draven scowled. He had a warm feeling in his stomach and wasn't quite sure about it. "That whole damn emotional episode, and the only thing you remember is that I called you 'baby'? Are you going soft on me, Abelard?"

Taylor chuckled, a dirty, low sound that went straight to Draven's groin. "I think the one thing I'm not around you, *Samuels*, is soft."

Draven stared at him.

Taylor grinned then his face sobered. "So…we've established that the voice I heard in the study, when Drew shot himself, was the wife. The wife who said she wasn't in the house at the time. What the hell do we do with that information?"

Draven shook his head. "Not us. Clay, my boss, can deal with this. We're going to go see him right now, pass on this information and he can take it further." He felt a shiver of apprehension at that. *This* story would take some telling.

"Your boss at Mortimer Investigations?" Taylor's eyes widened. "*The* Mortimer in the title?"

"The one and only. Clay will know exactly what needs to be done. He and Drew were sort of friends too, and business partners in a case I worked on. Clay was the one who originally uncovered the whole blackmail scenario. He knew something really bad had to happen for Drew to do what he did and he went digging. He moves in some…rather murky circles." Draven took a deep breath. "It will be a difficult job convincing him how we got the proof, but I'll give it a damned good try." His voice was grim. "He's pretty open-minded, so I hope it won't be too difficult. But you're coming with me. I might need you to do a demonstration."

Taylor's jaw dropped. His voice was disbelieving when he spoke. "You're taking me with you to your boss's office while you tell him a psychic guy…one that you're sleeping with… has evidence that contradicts the current state of events... gathered through solid police work I guess...and he needs to investigate something based on said crazy guy's input?" His voice rose. "And what do you mean, 'a demonstration'?"

Draven winced. Put like that it sounded crazy, and based on his last cock-up with Ian the Informant, he knew he was on shaky ground with Clay. Thinking about that, he hoped like hell Clay wouldn't bring it up in front of Taylor. Nothing like having the guy you're currently in bed with hearing about a past indiscretion and you sticking your dick where it didn't belong.

"I mean I might need you to show Clay what you can do." He ignored Taylor's exasperated snort and forged ahead. "It might not come to that, but I want to make sure I can convince him."

"Yeah, I'm sure he's going to listen to the likes of me. I'm sure you made your views about me well known back in the days when you thought I was a fraud." Taylor raised one sardonic eyebrow. "He probably thinks you've been cock whipped and you'll say anything to keep me sweet so you can continue to get some."

Draven felt his face flush. "Cock whipped?" he said haltingly. "What the hell are you talking about?"

Taylor smirked. "Well, I can't say pussy whipped because I don't have a..."

"Tay, I get it. Please don't even finish that sentence." Draven glared at an unrepentant Taylor. He thought his lover had certainly recovered from his little episode given the leer he had on his face. It made Draven want to pull the car over behind the hawthorn bushes growing on the side of the road and fuck him senseless. He manfully suppressed that impulse and rolled his eyes instead. "Now shut up a minute while I figure out how the hell I'm going to sell this to him."

He ignored Taylor's adorable pout and again reined in his desire to have his way with him. An hour and a half later, as he parked in front of the offices of Mortimer Investigations, in the rather pretty and scenic business park of Wembley, he still wasn't quite sure how he'd tackle the affair.

Taylor clambered out of the car. He'd been quiet on the way through, leaving Draven to figure things out and finally got bored and watched a film on his mobile phone. Draven could tell he was nervous.

"Are you sure this is a good idea, Draven?" Taylor asked hesitatingly. "I mean, this guy might think I'm a damn nutter, and maybe you might be putting your job at risk if he thinks you're one too. Maybe we should…"

Draven effectively shut him up by pulling Taylor toward him and sealing his mouth with his lips. Taylor gave a breathy moan and dissolved against Draven like a melting slab of Cadbury's. When Draven let him go, his lips were pink and swollen from the force of his kiss.

Draven grinned. "Now that you look truly fucked, let's go meet my boss."

He jauntily sped across the grass, blithely ignoring the No Treading On the Grass signs that were perched in fields of lush green, and made his way to the glassed entrance. He chuckled quietly as he saw Taylor make the longer way around using the path, the long-suffering expression on his face priceless.

Draven entered the building and smiled at the receptionist. "Hi, Shelley. How are you this afternoon?"

The pretty blonde woman behind the desk waved at Draven as Taylor came in behind him. Her eyes skipped Draven and alighted on Draven's man like a woman about to take a bite of a delicious chocolate-covered cherry. Draven thought she'd start drooling soon.

Shelly sat up, pushed her already perky boobs out and gave Taylor the full wattage of her smile. Draven felt a prickle of jealousy at the blatant come-hither action. She'd never done that to him and she didn't even know he was gay.

"Hi, Draven. Good to see you, it's been a while. And who is this gorgeous fellow then?" Her eyes lapped Taylor up, her interest obvious. "Wow, I'd like to get to know *you*. Are you going to be working with Draven?" Her tone was hopeful.

"He's with me, yes." Draven growled as he made his way to the lift and pushed the button with a short, stabbing action.

Let her take that comment any way she wants. Taylor is mine.

"I'm taking him to meet Clay. We have some business to discuss."

He didn't miss Taylor's smirk as he joined him at the lift after bestowing a dazzling, white-toothed smile at the receptionist. Draven saw her almost swoon in her chair and he fiercely jabbed the button again.

"Careful, Draven. I might even start to think you care about me," Taylor teased *sotto voce* as the lift doors opened and Draven propelled him inside. As the door closed, Draven pushed him back against the lift wall, pressing himself against an obviously amused Taylor.

"I don't like it when people come onto you," he muttered sulkily, his hands gripping Taylor's hips. "You're mine."

He hadn't meant to make such a statement but he couldn't help it. He was possessive by nature, he knew that, but he didn't want to scare Taylor off completely by being too Neanderthal.

However, knowing Taylor's propensity for being dominated now and then, he thought it might not go down too badly. He was right. Taylor's eyes darkened, a wet, pink tongue coming out to lick his lips unconsciously. A soft, peppermint-scented outtake of breath caressed Draven's skin.

Draven groaned as his cock sprang to life in his jeans. He stepped away quickly and adjusted himself. "Christ, stop that. Clay will notice. He notices everything."

Taylor laughed softly. "You started it, Mr. Caveman. Now you've got me hard. Do you think Clay will notice that too?"

Draven couldn't resist a look at Taylor's all-too-tight black jeans, losing his breath at the sight of the hard ridge lying left of the fabric.

"He can't possibly miss it." His voice was husky and he wondered whether they could delay seeing Clay for ten minutes while he resolved both of their problems in the fancy executive bathroom, for which he had a key card. His plan was thwarted as the lift doors opened and Clay Mortimer stood there, all one-hundred-and-eighty-odd pounds of muscle, tanned skin, black silver-grey streaked hair and attitude.

"Draven...and friend." Clay's voice was like warm honey, deep and melodious, unless it was busy ripping Draven a new one, which to be honest, was quite often. "What the hell are you doing here? I didn't expect to see you until next week. I was on my way out for a burger." A slight panic coated his voice with his next words. "Is everything okay with Jude?"

Draven nodded. "Jude's fine. That's not why I'm here."

Clay's eyes narrowed, and green eyes observed Draven carefully. Draven groaned inwardly as they dropped slightly toward

Draven's nether regions, then across to Taylor's, and then swung back up to him. His lips lifted slightly and Draven saw the amusement behind the cool facade.

"Been practising those weasel techniques, Dray?"

Draven pushed past his boss, out onto the landing. "Fuck. You," he expostulated as Taylor's jaw gaped open at that earthy retort. "It's urgent, and I need to speak to you, so maybe your McDonald's burger can wait." Clay had a habit of buying a Big Tasty almost every day. It was one of his "little pleasures," as he told everyone.

How Clay still managed to look so good, and keep the physique he had from his days as an SAS operative many years ago, Draven had no idea. Clay said that gym, hot sex and tequila were his secrets to maintaining his figure.

Draven walked into Clay's office at the end of the corridor. A fairly large space, with big picture windows looking out onto the green behind, it was filled with bookshelves, wall maps, and a wooden desk stood at one end, with two chairs in front.

Draven stood, staring out at the pond and fountain in the garden below. He was slightly nervous if truth be told. He'd worked with Clay for six years and always found the man to be fair, tough and supportive when it counted. Now Taylor was involved, he felt a little out of depth. Bluster and defensive techniques normally worked for him but today, he needed Clay to listen and accept what he was about to tell him. Clay and Taylor wandered into the office, Taylor looking very ill at ease, Clay simply striding to his chair and settling in comfortably as if he didn't have a care in the world. Draven mused wryly that telling his superior to fuck off probably hadn't been the best thing he could have done.

"Sooo, Dray." Clay swung his feet on top of his mahogany polished desk and sent a missile launch of green eyes his way. "You seem a little pissed off. Still smarting about that whole incident with Ian and me pulling you off the case? I thought you'd have gotten over that." He smirked, casting a sly glance at Taylor who was standing awkwardly at the window next to Draven.

Draven cut that one off at the pass. "Never mind Ian. That's old news." He ignored Taylor's speculative glance as he sat down in the chair in front of the huge desk. He motioned to Taylor to sit beside him in the other chair and Taylor shook his head.

"I'll stand, thanks." Draven noticed Taylor's Adam's apple bob as he swallowed, saw his clenching of fists and nervous licks of his lips.

He sighed. "Babe, stop looking like the guillotine's going to fall. It's going to be okay, I promise."

Clay's eyes widened, his dark eyebrows rising. "Babe? Well, well, well. What happened to the old animosity you felt for Mr. Abelard? This is a turn up for the books."

Draven took a deep breath, suppressing the impulse to snarl. "Clay, that's kind of what we're here to talk about."

Clay's eyebrows lifted further. "Your love life? Isn't that what got you into trouble in Dubrovnik? Putting your dick where it wasn't supposed to go?" He chuckled softly, but cast a softer glance at Taylor, as if commiserating. Taylor smiled uneasily.

Draven closed his eyes and counted to ten. "Clay, please let's forget that whole dick matter. And yes, Taylor and I are an item, okay? Now that's out of the way, do you want to me tell you some breaking news about Drew Whittaker's death?"

Clay stilled and moved his feet to the floor, then leaned forward, his whole demeanour changing. "Drew's death? Are you going to tell me it wasn't a suicide after all?"

Draven shook his head. "No, it was suicide. It's just that we have reason to believe that someone was with him when he pulled the trigger." He didn't miss Taylor's flinch at those words. "His wife lied when she said she wasn't home when it happened. She was there, right in the room with him. That makes me wonder why she lied, what she's covering up. Where there's smoke there's fire. You taught me that."

That wasn't the only thing Clay had taught Draven in the past. He was a mentor of note—if mentoring meant you learnt about 101 ways to kill a man, conduct covert operations and surveillance and be a sneaky bastard.

"I figured I'd tell you, and you could perhaps follow up on it. His wife is a basket case at the moment, and I guess she'd crack if you pushed her."

Taylor's indrawn breath made Draven realise that sounded callous, but he and Clay lived in a very different world than his lover. Sometimes nice wasn't an option when you were looking for the truth. He glanced at him and inclined his head slightly.

"I know that sounds cruel, Tay. But sometimes it's all you have to work with."

"I remember." Taylor said quietly. "You forget I've seen you at work."

Draven winced. Their encounter and his words at the site of little Bobby Meredith's body dump had come back to haunt him. "Yeah, so I was an arsehole then." He smiled, trying to reassure Taylor he wasn't any longer.

Clay laughed softly. "I like this one, Draven. He has balls. And I've never heard you admit you were an arsehole before to anyone." He nodded his head at Taylor in acknowledgement. "Well done, son. You seemed to have calmed the savage beast."

Taylor's face showed the sign of a slight grin and Draven felt a prickle of annoyance. "Can we stop the buddy bonding on my behalf please, and focus?" Both men swung their eyes to him. "There is a slight hitch with this information, though."

Taylor tensed, his arms wrapping around his chest, as he turned to look out of the window.

Clay's forehead creased. "Spill it. What's wrong with the information?" He was all matter of fact now, face set, voice harder, a man demanding answers and explanations. Clay Mortimer was a man Draven would never cross. Firstly, from a sense of sheer respect for him, and secondly, because he'd be hunted down like an animal and have his balls fed to him like culinary delicacies.

Draven took another deep breath as he prepared to speak.

"Because the information came from me." Taylor's voice echoed in the sudden stillness. "And it's not exactly reliable in any way you'd expect." Draven looked over at him. His lover's face was resolved, his arms unfolded and hanging by his sides as he regarded Clay with a stare of brown eyes that said he was about to have his say.

"You know who I am, obviously. So you know what I'm supposedly capable of. I have no doubt you have a dossier on me somewhere in here." He waved a hand around the room. "And Draven has seen what I can do first hand. I think I've made a believer out of him and I imagine you realise that's a fucking miracle based on his past impression of me."

Clay snorted but said nothing as he watched Taylor thoughtfully, his hands steepled together under his chin, elbows on his desk. Draven felt a prickle of guilt at Taylor's words.

"So we're here to tell you that I had a vision of Catherine Whittaker being present at the exact same time Drew shot himself. She cried out his name and I saw the back of her. She had nothing to do with the shooting, but she was there. We went back to the house and I confirmed the voice that I heard in the study was hers. I didn't get to see her, well, except from the funeral, and I only caught a glimpse of her then but the voice…it was her." His tone was challenging and Draven let out a breath, not realising he'd been holding it in. Clay was nodding sagely.

"Uh-huh." He stared at Draven. "And based on this…vision of your boyfriend's, you want me to investigate further, speak to the wife, accuse her of lying and see what comes out of it?"

Draven coughed uncomfortably. "Yeah. Basically." Inside, he was glowing at the term "boyfriend."

Simmer down, Draven. This isn't the time for warm and fuzzy. Hardened investigator, remember? Especially in front of Clay. You already slipped up calling Tay "babe."

Clay's green eyes glittered, his lips pursed. Then he shrugged. "Okay."

Draven felt as if he'd entered the Twilight Zone.

It couldn't possibly be that fucking easy.

Taylor looked gobsmacked too. He turned to stare at Draven.

"That's it?" Draven demanded. "You're going to just accept it like that?" He snapped his fingers. Clay leaned back in his chair, looking very relaxed for a man who'd just been told that his operative's psychic boyfriend had important news to share that he'd gleaned from a vision.

"Sure," he drawled, eyes shining with suppressed amusement. "You forget, Draven, when you used to mouth off about this young man, I didn't really agree with you. Just let you rant. I've seen Mr. Abelard's file, spoken to people who've been on the receiving end of his abilities—fairly senior people who aren't generally very receptive about such things. They vouched for him all those years ago in the Bobby Meredith case. And so have others where your young man's abilities have been useful." He shrugged. "So I can afford to give him the benefit of the doubt in this one."

"You've been talking to my friend Rick Grant," Taylor mused slowly, regarding Clay narrowly. "And probably Rick's uncle, a police detective called Tate Williams. Rick says he's always been very supportive of what I do." A fond look crossed his face.

At the mention of the names, Clay's face closed up and his lips thinned. Draven recognised that tell as being something Clay wouldn't talk about and he wondered what he was trying to hide. He also wondered who the hell Rick Grant was and whether he was the one causing the sappy look on Taylor's face. He'd heard of Tate Williams; everyone in law enforcement had heard of him. He was a dyed-in-the-wool police officer who'd been forced to take early retirement after a horrific shooting. He'd been shot by a vengeful ex-con three times on his way home from his local gym and was lucky to have survived.

"Perhaps," Clay murmured diffidently. "We move in the same circles." He waved a hand. "Anyway, just be glad I haven't put you through the mill on this one." He smirked. "I bet Dray here had you all primed and ready to blast away to give me some sort of 'demonstration' to prove your worth?"

Draven's face flushed and Clay cackled loudly. "God, will you look at him. I can't believe you would have staged something like that for me."

Taylor laughed softly and Draven glared at him. "I didn't think you'd be this receptive. I thought…"

A mobile rang shrilly from the confines of Clay's trouser pocket and he held up a hand, forestalling Draven's words.

"I need to take this," he said quickly and stood up and walked over the window as he answered the phone. "Hey, baby. I've been waiting for your call. What did the doctor say?"

A man's voice could be heard from the other side and Draven grinned at Taylor's look of disbelief as he mouthed the word "Baby?"

As long as Draven had known Clay, the one Achilles heel he knew he possessed was the man in his life. No one knew who he was as Clay was as cagey as all hell about it. Draven wouldn't pry either. Clay's private life was his own. Clay was a kitten where *he* was concerned—soft and playful. Each time Draven heard him on the phone to him, Draven marvelled at the change in the man.

Whoever the man was on the other end of the phone, he was lucky to have the devotion and the heart of a man like Clay Mortimer.

Draven stood up and walked over to Taylor, whispering in his ear. "What, you think you're the only one that gets called that?"

"I just never expected it from him, that's all. Hell, we gay guys need our own damn county. Gaymanshire, or something like that." Taylor sniggered and Draven sighed.

"Funny man. But it's not a bad idea. It beats having to figure out whether the guy sitting next to me swings my way or not."

"Yeah, well, you don't need to worry about that anymore do you?" Taylor said silkily.

"Depends," Draven said airily. "On who and what Rick Grant is to you."

Taylor's breath hitched and he looked a little apprehensive. "No one you need worry about," he said, his hands running through his hair. "Rick and I used to have a thing but that was over a while ago." He smirked. "I'd like to hear that stray dick story sometime too. Anyway, are we exclusive? It's not something we've talked about, is it?"

Draven's stomach clenched. Taylor was right. They hadn't discussed their current situation and perhaps he was reading more into it than Taylor was. He felt a twinge of pique at that thought, that he might be more invested.

I never thought I'd have this worry, he thought as he clenched his fingers. *I'm normally the one backing off.*

Taylor opened his mouth to say something, a slight look of worry on his face. At that moment, Clay turned around and strode over to them. Taylor's mouth closed but he glanced at Draven curiously.

Draven wondered what he'd been about to say.

"Where were we?" Clay muttered, his tone distracted and his face pinched. Whatever news he'd received didn't seem good. "Oh yes. You were both just leaving so I can get home. With my McDonald's."

Draven stared at him. "So that's it then? Are you going to speak to Catherine Whittaker and see what comes of it?"

"I said I would, didn't I?" Clay scowled. "Your boyfriend there seems convinced so I'll give him the benefit of the doubt. Once." He smiled wolfishly at Taylor, who blinked. "If it all turns out to be complete bullshit, I'll get my gun out and shoot the two of you." His voice was grim as he went to his desk and started moving papers, looking for something. Draven saw Taylor blanch beneath his coffee-coloured skin.

"Stop being so fucking melodramatic, Clay," he muttered. "We'll let you get off then. You will call me, let me know how it all turns out?"

Clay turned distractedly. "What? Oh, yes. I'll call you if I have anything to say." He held up a bunch of keys in triumph. "Bloody things always get lost under the damn paperwork." His expression changed as he regarded Draven carefully. "I meant to ask, are things still the same with Jude? Have you made any decision yet?"

Draven's body stiffened. "No." His tone was clipped. "I wish the fuck everyone would let me be on this. Taylor's the only one who doesn't seem to push me on it. And that's the way I want it to stay. It's not his worry. It's my problem to deal with."

Taylor shifted on his feet and glanced down at the floor as he frowned.

Clay sighed. "Not pushing, Dray. Just concerned. Sorry I brought it up. Give him a kiss from me when you see him next." His eyes shadowed as he glanced at Taylor then back at Draven. "I know it's not easy, son. Just go with your gut. That always stood me in good stead when I was in the service. Follow your instincts."

He motioned at them both impatiently. "Now, be gone, the two of you. I have somewhere I need to be." His voice was pained and Draven knew him well enough to know the man was hurting.

He looked at Taylor and shrugged. "I think we've overstayed our welcome. I suppose I should get you home and then get home myself. It's been a long day."

Taylor's eyes narrowed and Draven thought he looked a little pissed off. He wondered fleetingly what he'd said wrong. Again. "Clay, thanks for the chat. I'll expect to hear from you soon."

Clay was looking at his mobile intently and he didn't even look up as he waved a hand. "Yep. See you guys."

Summarily dismissed, Draven led the way out of the office, Taylor behind him. Taylor was quiet as they took the lift down and walked to the car. It was a very different journey from the one up to the office. When they were in the vehicle with seat belts on and Draven had started the car, he sighed and looked at Taylor.

"Out with it," he said quietly. "What's bugging you?"

Taylor's lips pressed together mutinously. "Never mind," he said shortly. "It doesn't really matter. Just take me home."

"Something's upset you, Tay." Draven felt the need to push.

"I'm fine, really." Draven could see Taylor was anything but fine as he leaned his head against the seat rest and closed his eyes, as if shutting out all possibility of conversation.

"I think that went well, considering," he murmured, hoping that he'd draw Taylor out.

"Uh-huh."

"Clay's good at manipulating people, getting them to paint themselves into a corner. If anyone can get to the truth, that man can."

"Okay."

Draven felt the prickle of irritation down his spine at the monosyllabic replies. He tried valiantly one last time.

"I mean, there must have been a reason for her to lie, and while it won't bring Drew back, maybe it has some bearing on his suicide. Maybe she knows something about the blackmailer."

"Yep."

Draven exploded as he weaved in and out of traffic, taking care not to drive too fast. "Christ, Taylor, I'm trying to make conversation here. What the hell is wrong with you?"

Taylor's eyes opened and flashed dark lasers of anger at him.

"Excuse me if I don't feel too chatty. I'm not sure we're on the same page here. Do you know the reason I don't push you on the subject of your brother?" His jaw clenched. "Because I don't seem to really have a say in anything about it. One, I only found out about it today even though I've been asking you what's up for weeks. Two, I asked you to take me to see him and you ignored me. Three, based on one and two, you've given me the bare bones of that tragedy but I doubt you'll let me in to share it with you so we can talk about the *decision* you have to make, whatever the fuck that means. It's 'not my worry,' after all."

He folded his arms across his chest, hugging himself. Emotion vibrated from his lean body like a taut violin string being plucked.

Draven's eyes widened at Taylor's growing anger as his fingers clenched on the steering wheel. He barked back. "Maybe I don't solicit your advice because we might not be 'exclusive' as you reminded me. Maybe the story is more for someone who means to stick around, not someone who thinks this thing we have is just 'fun.' Maybe I'm just another 'regular.'"

No sooner had the words left his mouth, he regretted them. A sick feeling welled in his stomach.

Way to go, you prick. God, that must be just about the worst thing you could have said to him.

Taylor's eyes widened and his face paled. "I was joking back there about the whole exclusive thing, Draven. I didn't think we had to talk about it to realise…" His voice cut off and he closed his eyes, his face suddenly weary. The defeat in his face worried Draven more than if Taylor had hit him again. Something he'd probably not blame him for. "You know what, just take me home. That dinner you promised me tonight will have to wait."

Draven felt another twinge of guilt at the thought he'd forgotten his promise to take Taylor out.

"Taylor, I'm sorry. I shouldn't have said that."

Taylor's lips thinned and he stared out the front window of the car, ignoring Draven. His fingers were curled into tight fists.

"I don't want to talk. Just fucking take me home." His tone was tight and controlled.

Draven heard the warning in Taylor's voice and decided to let it go. For now.

They drove in awkward silence the rest of the way home. Draven stopped outside Taylor's house and switched off the engine, and Taylor clipped off his seatbelt and was out the car before the engine had even stopped purring.

"Thanks for the day trip," he said flatly from outside the open car door. "Are you going to go see your brother tonight?"

Draven hesitated then nodded. "Yes. I'll probably grab something to eat and shower first though. Visiting hours are later." His mouth went dry. "Tay, I…"

"I hope it all goes all right with him. G'night, Draven. I'll see you around." Taylor closed the door with an air of finality and strode toward his front door. Draven could only watch helplessly as he disappeared inside.

*****

Taylor got home and slumped straight into the easy chair in the lounge. He bit his fingernails as he sat in the semi darkness, with only the faint glow of a new fish tank lighting up the room. He shook his head in bemusement.

When the hell did that get there? Shows you just how much I've been home lately. Not.

He knew it had to be Leslie's and he grinned faintly at the thought despite the turmoil in his gut and the ache in his chest.

Every pet that Leslie had brought into the house to date had either died or "disappeared." The pet goldfish, Rollo—a gift from an old flame who'd won it at a fun fair coconut shy competition—had been found floating belly up in his bowl one morning. Leslie had shrieked the place down, seemingly overcome with grief. Then there had been the pet spider that he'd "adopted" when it was found in the bathtub. Taylor and Eddie were in favour of flushing it down the toilet. Leslie however had decided it deserved mercy and had kept in a shoebox in his room for the princely time of a whole two days before it had mysteriously "disappeared."

Given the fact that Eddie hadn't seemed too concerned at the possibility of a spider lurking around the house (and him being very afraid of said arachnids) and wearing a satisfied smirk during the frantic search of couches, cushions and cupboards, Taylor had a feeling it had been relegated to the great unknown somewhere, probably a sewer. And then there had been the bird Leslie found in his room, with a broken wing. Gloria Gaynor had been nursed back to health, staying the longest out of all Leslie's guests, until one day, in a fit of sheer indulgence, Leslie had perched her on the windowsill to watch her brothers and sisters enjoy the great outdoors, and she'd promptly flown away. He'd been devastated and it had taken half a dozen cups of chamomile tea for Taylor to calm him down. Not to mention Taylor's promise of a new pair of Ted Baker heels that Leslie had his eye on, something he could ill afford at the time.

Taylor huffed and regarded the colourful fish in the tank with jaundiced eyes. The minute Draven had uttered the words "It's not his worry. It's my problem to deal with," Taylor's temper had flared. Already under some stress from the morning's emotional meeting at the Threadcourts' house, coupled with meeting Draven's boss for the first time, his already fragile psyche had been on high alert. Hearing Draven so brazenly declare he didn't think Taylor needed to be involved in his affairs had really given him the hump. Then taking that throwaway comment about being exclusive out of context, and the barb about being a "regular"—well, that had really been the final straw.

He'd never thought a chest could hurt so much, as his had tightened and his heart had thumped out of control. So now he sat grumpily ensconced in the worn chair, eating his fingers and wondering what to do next. There was no way he was going to call Draven any time soon. The bastard had gone too far.

If he wants me, he can come and find me. I'm not making the first move again. And when he does, he's going to pay for those words. My mission is going to be to drive him crazy. The man won't know what's hit him. Let him see what he's missing when he's being a prick.

The thought of getting his own back on Draven soothed the turmoil in his soul and he closed his eyes and leaned back. He was bone tired.

Taylor dreamt. Not the blood-soaked nightmares of the past but something that felt even a little more disturbing in that it soaked into his bones and sent tiny tendrils of insidious emotions into his psyche. What disturbed him more was that those tendrils were infused with hope. His normal visions of dismembered children, desperate people with violence in their souls and those who simply latched onto him like leeches intent on sucking him dry were long gone. Instead, there was softness, eagerness, a whisper in his mind that it was time to go, time to move on and a gentle urging to make him listen. Focus. Warmth enveloped him instead of the cold dread he was used to, and wrapped comforting arms around his still body, beguiling him with the promise of an ending of something that had dragged on far too long. In his sleep, Taylor smiled softly then nodded as the voice told him that he had to help.

When he woke up, he was crying. Silent tears rolled down his cheeks; his breath was heavy, his chest aching from something that felt like both loss and relief. He sat up in bed, reaching wondering fingers to his cheeks to feel the slick wetness on his face. Taylor drew a shuddering breath as he reached for his shirt and wiped his eyes. He could still hear the echo of the words in his head, resonating in the cold, dark room.

Save me. Tell him to let me go.

Chapter 9

The hospital was silent as Draven sat beside his brother's bedside in the critical care ward. An overhead light above him flickered, and Draven, in his morbid frame of mind, wondered whether someone, somewhere was dying and the flickering light was a reflection of the ebb and flow of life.

He sighed and passed a hand over tired, strained eyes. He heard the soft murmuring from people at the nurse's station just outside the ward, and saw quiet purposefulness in the movements of the personnel on call as they moved around. It was late at night and only a few visitors still lingered in the corridors. He'd come straight from his time with Taylor, needing to see his brother.

He shifted in his uncomfortable chair and lifted his arms above his head, stretching. Jude slept on, his body still, his face never changing. Draven has helped the nurses move him, rub his skeletal limbs and he'd been horrified to see the worsening state of his brother's body. Doctor Frederick had quietly assured him that everything was being done, but before Draven's eyes, his little brother was wasting away before him.

He reached out and touched a stringy, greasy piece of hair that fell across Jude's pale brow. "Hey, there, little bro," he whispered. "Can you hear me?" He asked that question a half a dozen times in the hours he visited Jude. He'd never had a response, no inkling that Jude heard him at all. "I met someone. His name is Taylor. I think you'd like him. He reminds me of you, a little. He's also damn cheeky, causes me grey hairs and doesn't listen to a word I say. I also think I cocked up any hope of a relationship tonight." He laughed softly but there was tinge of despair in it. "We have this thing going, though, and guess what? He's a damn psychic. Yep, you never thought you'd hear your big brother confess to that one, huh?"

He gently stroked Jude's thin arm. The skin was warm, soft, and Draven's eyes prickled. The only thing he had left of him was the feel of his brother's flesh beneath his fingertips. It was the only indication he had that his brother was still there. It was scant comfort when he remembered how active Jude had been as a kid. He'd always been trouble, always enterprising, sometimes to the point of disobedience and devilry. At the time Draven had seen it as rebelling, as flouting Draven's authority when he'd been left to babysit Jude. Now, Draven wanted that back more than anything in the world. He continued stroking Jude's arm.

"I miss you, sweetheart. Every fucking day I miss you, your smile, and your voice. I miss those crazy impersonations you used to do of Pepé Le Pew and Bart Simpson. I miss you singing Bruce Springsteen tunes and playing air guitar." His voice cracked and tears were now rolling freely down his face. "I miss our stupid ice cream challenges to see which one of us got a brain freeze first. God, I miss everything, Jude. I just…"

His voice could no longer express everything he missed, everything that had been taken away from them both, but mostly, from a young boy who would never become a young man. "Christ, I don't know what to do…I don't know."

His nose was streaming now, as he sobbed, bowing his head to sniffle against Jude's side, where the respirator puffed and breathed for him, making his thin chest rise and fall. Draven had never felt such agony, such finality. He knew he was nearing the end of the road with Jude. That fact, coupled with the thought of knowing that he had to make the decision that would break his heart and leave him shattered and torn, made him want to close his eyes, hug his knees to his chest and hibernate in a dark place.

The enormity of the task ahead of him swept through him like cold Siberian air, chilling his bones to the marrow and making him wonder if his heart would ever beat again.

There was a swell of air beside him, like a bubble of warmth and he looked up, eyes red, and blurred, thinking someone was beside him. His scalp prickled and his hair stirred, as if someone had passed by and touched him. There was no one there and he knew it was his own longing and desperation that was creating these illusions.

"Are you there, Jude?" he whispered. "Can you hear me? I wish you could tell me what you want, tell me whether you're in pain. That damn doctor of yours says you aren't but what the hell do they know? They aren't you. They aren't stuck in this fucking bed, wasting away, so how can they say that?" He used the sleeve of his long-sleeved shirt to wipe his eyes and grabbed a box of tissues from the bedside table to blow his nose. "I want to do the right thing, little brother. I want to make sure I do what's best for you and I don't know what that is."

His body shuddered and he sniffed again, trying to clear his blocked nose. "Taylor's the only person keeping me sane at the moment and God knows I don't tell him much about this whole thing. He doesn't understand that I don't want to mess him up; he's going through enough stuff of his own what with all the shitty deaths he sees and the feelings he has to live with. How can I lay this on him as well? I don't even understand it all myself."

Draven remembered a conversation he'd had with Taylor. They'd been huddled in bed, warm under the covers and talk had turned to what Taylor did and how. Draven had tucked stray strands of hair behind his lover's ears as they talked.

"I've never believed in this whole life after death before and to me, this is such a reach to believe that there's something else out there, after we leave this world. I still can't process it."

Taylor had sighed tiredly. "It's strange for me too. Yes, I know I feel things, see things, but that's a world removed from what just happened. I guess if I believe in feeling the spirits or energy of people who've died and I can feel their pain, see their last moments, it's not such a huge stretch to believe that people go somewhere else when they die. Energy, soul, spirit, whatever it is. It's not for *us* to figure out, Draven. It's ours to either accept or not. It's about taking a leap of faith."

He'd wrapped warm arms around Draven's waist. Draven had leaned back into him, as Taylor nuzzled his neck, smelling his man's fragrance and revelling in it. "It doesn't matter where *it* is. To every person, it might be a different place, or a world, or a realm we don't even know about. To people who believe in heaven, that's their place, I suppose. It's wherever anyone wants to go when they leave this world."

Those words still haunted him.

"Draven?" The quiet voice behind him made him start and he turned swiftly to see calm, brown eyes regarding him with compassion. Sister Alison Maduna was a fixture in this ward and her quiet, competent presence was always welcoming to all, but especially to Draven. He'd sobbed against her ample bosom more times than he'd like to admit, as she patted his back and treated him like the mother he'd lost. The reassuring West African nurse had been there for him through the past three years of hell and Draven didn't know what he'd have done without her.

"I thought you were off duty tonight," he croaked as he tried valiantly to dry his eyes and compose himself. She moved over to him and patted his shoulder, her warm hands on his body giving him comfort.

"No, I changed shifts with Julia. She had a family emergency so I took her shift." She pulled over another chair with a scrape of legs against the tiled floor and set her ample buttocks down beside him. "How are you doing, baby?"

Draven waved a hand. "As you can see, I'm fine." His voice was muffled, as his he struggled to breathe through his stuffed nose.

She smiled. "Having a bad night, huh? Is our little man giving you grief, back chatting perhaps?" She reached over and tenderly stroked Jude's cheek. "Hey, you little rapscallion, stop making your brother cry. He's supposed to be a big bad ass and I come in and find him in tears? Shame on you, baby. Shame on you."

Her teasing tone to his still brother made Draven smile wanly. "Yeah, I wish, Ally. I'd take that, you know? Take anything he wanted to give me." His voice broke again but this time the tears stayed away. Draven had cried enough tonight.

Alison cuffed his jaw line gently with large, warm fingers. "I know. I wish that too. You've been so brave through this, honey. I wish I could do more for you, you know? I wish I could wave a magic wand and make this all go away. Bring him back."

Her voice was sad and the unspoken words lay between them like a freight train about to plunge off a mountain.

And you know that's the one thing I can't do.

She sat with Draven, both of them lost in their own thoughts. Draven took comfort in having this woman by his side, the one constant in Jude's situation the whole time he'd been there. They had become friends of a kind inside these antiseptic walls of both grief and joy.

Finally she stood up and placed a soft kiss on the top of his head. She went to Jude and did the same then the nurse checked the leads and wires keeping his brother alive, ran a critical eye over his body and checked the chart at the foot of the bed. When she had finally finished she turned to Draven, who'd been watching the activity with weary eyes.

"There. He's comfortable enough. Aren't you, honey?" Her hands caressed Jude's arm. "Maybe you should go home, get some sleep, Draven. It's been a long night."

Draven shook his head. "No, I'm staying here tonight. I'll sleep in the chair."

Alison nodded. "I know when your mind's made up, you can't be swayed. I'll get one of the night nurses to bring you a blanket and a cup of coffee. Have you eaten?"

"Not hungry. I had a sandwich earlier." The sandwich had been two tasteless pieces of bread with pale slices of anaemic ham and soggy tomato between them.

Alison tut-tutted. "I know your idea of food, Draven, and it scares me. I'll see if I can get you something a little more substantial. It was chicken and vegetables tonight and I have to say, it wasn't too shabby." She grinned. "I had some myself so it must have been okay. I'll be back in a while."

Alison disappeared out of the room. Draven sighed and got comfortable in the chair where he'd probably spend the night.

Best get hunkered down. Tonight I'm here for the long haul.

He thought of Taylor, who was probably not even in bed yet. His heart ached but he couldn't bring himself to call him. Not yet. He was still too raw inside and he needed a little time to get his head right. He was no good to anyone at the moment, least of all himself.

*****

One week later and Draven was feeling the effects of not seeing Taylor. He missed the man like a limb that had been removed. The night he'd come home from visiting Jude, he'd had a call in the early hours of the next morning. He'd been sent on another assignment out of the country by Clay, on an assignment that had been "urgent and life threatening," with the fate of the nation hanging in the balance. Clay could often be rather drama ridden himself. Draven had been handed an itinerary, a plane ticket to Lithuania and a grinning admonishment from his boss to keep his dick in his pants this time. Draven had texted Taylor from the airport to let him know he was going away for a while but there had been no response. His subsequent texts and phone calls had been ignored, apart from one text that Taylor had sent back after Draven's last one, the day before he arrived back in the UK.

Tay, I'm back in London tomorrow. Can I see you to talk?

Taylor's response had been short. *Call me. We'll see.*

Draven had scowled at that terse reply, not being a man to chase after what he wanted but the fact Taylor was willing to perhaps get together had made him feel a little better. Of course, his innate sense of bloody-mindedness made him wonder if he *would* call his lover.

Taylor isn't the only stubborn bastard.

The case in Lithuania had been fairly straightforward, and the young hacker genius who operated out there, who had been stealing millions from a state-based charity in Russia—ostensibly based out there to help refugees—had been given an ultimatum.

Work for us or go to prison. That had basically been Draven's brief. The youngster, only twenty-three years old, had talents that Mortimer Investigations would find extremely useful. The money he'd stolen and amassed in an offshore bank account had been returned to the charity who had only been too relieved that it had found its way back to worry about pursuing justice for the hacker. Tomas Pavlis had vehemently defended his theft, telling Draven with glittering blue eyes that the funds were not being used for the purpose for which they were intended and Russian human rights violations made it his mission to relieve them of their funds.

It had taken some doing but Draven had managed to convince Tomas that now they'd tracked him down, handing the young hacker over to the Russian authorities had not been in anyone's best interests and his skills would be better suited to working with Mortimer Investigations. Tomas had grudgingly seen the light and left with Draven to London on a business class ticket. Draven had been glad to deposit the rather feisty and argumentative young man into the clutches of Draven's boss once they'd arrived in London.

The first thing he'd done when arriving back in England was visit Jude. He'd had daily reports from then nurses on how he was doing, the words "No change" being most of what was conveyed. Draven had an irrational fear that something would happen to Jude when he was out of the country and the nursing staff were used to his paranoia. Clay was a ready conduit to how his brother was faring, as he visited often too.

Draven had also given into temptation and called Taylor after he'd seen Jude. Taylor had sounded tired, and a little cool, but he'd agreed to meet Draven at Galileo's for dinner that night. Not only did Draven want to mend bridges but he also had other news to impart, news that he hoped might take some of the weight of Drew's death off Taylor's shoulders and make him feel better about the whole affair.

"Sitting on your own? Is Taylor late?" came the drawl from behind him. Draven turned to see Gideon, immaculately dressed as ever, smiling at him. Luckily he didn't have Eddie with him. Gideon's red-headed lover wasn't particularly enamoured of Draven. He always seemed very keen on sticking a skewer or some other kitchen implement in Draven's flesh.

"Only by a few minutes. We agreed eight p.m., it's just a few minutes past." For a moment, Draven felt a surge of panic that Taylor had decided not to come after all.

"Speak of the devil…" Gideon murmured, his eyes glinting with amusement. Draven followed the direction of his friend's eyes and held his breath on seeing Taylor. His lover (at least he hoped he still was) looked as sexy as hell. He wore tight-fitting black chinos, a deep red shirt open to the chest, and his wayward curls were swept back behind his ears. He looked like something out of *Pirates of the Caribbean*, wild and untamed, dark eyes observing Draven closely as he approached the table.

"Wow, someone has got it bad," teased Gideon. "Might I suggest you shut your mouth a little? I doubt he's going to put his dick in it right here and now."

"Fuck off," Draven growled, even as he tried to control the rising urge in his pants. "I hate you sometimes. Haven't you got a restaurant to run?"

Gideon sniggered. "He does look *very* tempting…" he drawled. "If I didn't have a jealous red head waiting for me, I might have a taste myself."

Draven knew he was joking but that still didn't stop him from snarling. "He's mine. You can't bloody have him."

Gideon tut-tutted. "Possessive to the last. Now you know how I feel about Eddie. I seem to remember you laughing at me one time and telling me that I was like a rabid dog pissing on his territory. It's not so funny when the shoe's on the other foot, eh?"

He leaned in close as Taylor got to the table and glanced at them both uncertainly. "Don't fuck it up," Gideon mouthed in his ear. "This one's a keeper."

He straightened up and pulled out Taylor's chair, waving for him to sit down.

"Taylor, welcome. Draven here was starting to worry you'd changed your mind." Draven glared at him.

Gideon ignored the laser-like stare. "Can I get you a drink?" he asked Taylor.

Taylor sat down and stared between them, looking a little confused. "Uhm, a Corona please."

Gideon waved an expansive hand and gave a mini bow. "Coming up. I'll bring you another whisky, Dray. I'll send someone over to take your food order later." He turned and walked away then turned back as if he'd forgotten something. "Oh, and Taylor, Eddie said he'd cut off your balls if you didn't say hello to him while you were here. He's going to pop out later and say hi."

He sauntered off and Draven rolled his eyes. "Great," he muttered. "As long as he doesn't come out with a damn meat cleaver, I'll be fine."

"What?" Taylor said, perplexed.

"Nothing." Draven finished off the dregs of his whisky. "It's just your buddy Eddie seems to have it in for me."

Taylor smirked slightly and Draven was glad to see it. It meant Taylor perhaps wasn't so mad at him if he could do that sexy movement with his mouth.

"And I always thought Eddie liked arseholes," Taylor murmured slyly. "Just goes to show you that people can still surprise you."

Draven leaned forward across the table, ignoring that quip. "I tried to tell you I was sorry for what I said," he growled. "But every text or phone call went unanswered, and you damn well ignored me."

Taylor shrugged, and Draven's eyes were drawn to the way Taylor's body made that simple gesture look like full-blown seduction. The man had an unconscious beauty that made Draven want to rip the red shirt off his beautiful shoulders and fuck him across the table. His dick still hadn't quiet subsided from his earlier sighting and that thought brought it alive again like the beast of Frankenstein, electricity surging through flesh and blood rising into places he'd forgotten he had. It had been too long since he'd gotten laid.

While in Lithuania, he'd been to a couple of secret gay bars frequented by people in the know, and been hit on by numerous men, but he'd not taken one of them up on their offers. For some frustrating reason, he'd thought of Taylor every time a man's fingers had brushed his crotch, or squeezed his arse, or as one man had done, stuck his tongue in his ear as if giving him an aural clean.

He had gone back to his hotel room horny and frustrated and jacked off to the memory of Taylor riding his cock like a beautiful wild horse, all sleek skin and lithe muscle. That alone had been the extent of his sexual endeavours in the past week. Now the man in his fantasies regarded him with liquid brown eyes as his hands idly stroked the silky edges of the shirt lying across his chest. Every so often they'd pause and dwell on the caramel-coloured skin beneath, as Taylor's delicate finger tips caressed his own flesh and Draven's eyes were drawn to those movements like a starving dog to a meaty bone.

He finally managed to pull his eyes away to look up and saw Taylor staring at him in amusement, his eyes darkened. He licked his lips, pink tongue wetting full, luscious lips, another gesture that sent Draven's cock into a tail spin. There was no mistaking the look of avarice in Taylor's eyes or the intent in the movements he made.

The little bastard is doing it deliberately. He's trying to drive me fucking crazy.

Draven admitted it was working.

"So, your little trip to Lithuania. Did it all go well?" Taylor smiled at the waitress placing his beer on the table and she grinned at him as she gave Draven his whisky. Taylor picked up the bottle, wrapping lips around the top, lime and all, and then with his tongue, he pushed the lime deeply into the bottle. Draven had never seen that particular trick performed before but the thought of that lucky bottleneck enjoying that gifted tongue in Taylor's mouth was making his groin ache. Taylor lifted the bottle, exposing the smooth column of his throat and the Adam's apple that bobbed as he drank down his first taste of beer. He made a small noise of contentment, similar to the one Draven had heard before when he was fucking him, and he leaned back in his chair, trying to get more comfortable. He took a slug of his drink and was not surprised to see he'd drank nearly half of it when he put the drink down. Taylor's eyes glinted when he saw what was left and he lowered his bottle with a satisfied sigh.

"Nothing like the first beer of the day," he murmured. "*You* must have been thirsty." He waved at the whisky. "Anyway, where was I? Oh, yes, your business trip. Meet anyone special out there?"

"No," Draven rumbled. "It wasn't that sort of trip. Purely business."

Taylor raised an eyebrow. "I thought you had a habit of mixing business with pleasure?"

Draven's face tightened. "It was just business. Are you going to bust my chops all night or are we going to enjoy dinner like two normal people without the sarcasm and jibes?"

Taylor opened his mouth to answer but a tornado chose that moment to approach their table and attack Draven's dinner date. Eddie Tripp beamed as he dragged Taylor to his feet and enveloped him in a lanky-armed bear hug. A noisy, smacking kiss was delivered to Taylor's lips, a kiss that left what looked like traces of flour on Taylor's mouth.

"Tay, you're looking good, my friend. Oops, sorry, got some stuff on your face." Eddie licked his fingers and wiped the offending smear from Taylor's mouth. "There, got it. So how have you been?"

He turned to look at Draven and tough as he was, the malevolent stare focused on him turned Draven's blood to ice. Eddie looked like Maleficent, albeit with red hair and green piercing eyes.

"I see you two are still together then. The rumour mill is right for once." He turned around and his fingers poked Draven in the chest. "I hope you're treating him right because you know if you don't, I'm coming after you."

Draven was speechless.

How the hell does Gideon sleep at night with this feisty virago in his bed? He must have one eye open when he does.

Taylor was laughing quietly. "Eddie, baby, it's fine, honest. Draven and I are here having dinner, that's all. No need to get all snarky with him."

Draven knew Eddie wasn't too fond of him after the incident in which he'd made Taylor pass out in the restaurant, but he thought he'd have gotten over it by now. He was glad Taylor was defending him though.

"Hmm." Eddie didn't look convinced. "Is he treating you okay, though, is what I want to know."

Taylor looked at Draven. "I'm not sure yet. It's still under advisement."

He shrugged and Draven felt a prickle of unease that he wasn't out of the woods yet. He watched mesmerised as Taylor's lips once again ran around the rim of his bottle and he looked at Draven from eyes that definitely promised...something. Draven wasn't quite sure what it was.

"Well, you know where to find me if you need back-up," Eddie muttered. He made to move away then turned around again and Draven saw the evil glint in his green eyes. "Oh, by the way, did Markie call you? You know, that guy we met in the bar the other night that you gave your number to?"

Draven's chest tightened. It was difficult to act nonchalant when the slow burn of jealousy inflamed him. He pressed his lips together, waiting to see what Taylor's reply was.

Taylor nodded. "Yeah, he did, the next day. He asked me to go with him to the Nickelback concert next week." He set his drink down idly, tracing a pattern on the frosty outside of the bottle. Draven saw it looked like a set of balls and a penis. He glared at Taylor whose lips held the trace of a slow smile as his eyes focused on his circling finger.

"And?" Eddie demanded impatiently. "Christ, it's like pulling teeth with you."

"I told him it depends." Taylor's eyes lifted to meet Draven's and he was under no illusions that it depended on him and what would happen next. Whether things got better and Taylor forgave him for his outburst.

Eddie snorted. "Good. It always helps to keep your options open." He cast a fiery glance at Draven, who stared back. "Anyway, let me go before the boss fires my arse." He grinned and Draven couldn't help noticing that it really was a rather attractive one, making the man seem much more approachable. "Then I'd have to convince him to give my job back somehow."

"I doubt you'd have any problem convincing 'the boss' to take you back," Taylor remarked with a laugh.

Eddie chuckled. "Probably not. Have a good evening, Tay. I'll call you tomorrow." He gave his friend's shoulder a tight squeeze with an evil glare in Draven's direction and a warning to "treat Taylor like something precious" or he'd kick his arse. He narrowly avoided knocking into a waiter passing by with a plate full of food. Taylor sniggered and stared after him fondly.

"He's really protective of you, isn't he?" Draven said softly. "It doesn't bode well for me if I put a foot wrong, but I'm glad someone has your back." He desperately wanted to ask Taylor if he intended going to the Nickelback concert with Markie but didn't want to come across too desperate. He'd try another tactic.

"So you like Nickelback then? I didn't know that. I enjoy their music as well. Chad Kroeger is pretty much a genius."

Taylor nodded. Draven couldn't help thinking he looked rather amused.

"Yes, I love their music. Rock and roll and all that angst-fuelled testosterone in the music. It's just good, dirty fun to listen to. Maybe we should take in a concert together sometime."

Draven couldn't help himself. "Yeah? So you don't want to go with that other guy then?"

Taylor laughed softly and the sound sent chills down Draven's back and made his cock push against his trousers.

"No, Dray, I don't want to go with Markie. I'd rather go with you."

Those words gave Draven hope that things were about to take a turn for the better.

He was still feeling that warm glow of hope when they got back to Draven's house after a very innuendo-laden and hasty dinner and Taylor began ripping his clothes off the moment the door shut behind them. Draven took that as a sign that he'd been forgiven, which had been hinted at earlier with the constant teasing activity in the restaurant as Taylor made love with his mouth to some sort of chocolate dessert and his toes had kept creeping up to rub Draven's balls under the table. He'd also not wanted to spoil Taylor's unexpected good mood by telling him the latest news on Drew's death. Having his balls rubbed was a far better plan.

Draven was happy to oblige now in getting his kit off but he was determined that there was only one way this evening was going to go down. Once they were both naked, he took charge and heaved a protesting, but chuckling Taylor onto his shoulder in a fireman's lift, and stalked into the bedroom. Taylor was thrown onto the bed as

Draven followed him, crawling toward him on hands and knees like a hunting leopard.

He lowered his body on top of the struggling Taylor, pinning his hands above his head with one strong hand, and grinding his ready cock against Taylor's own hardness. The struggling ceased and instead, a whimper of need escaped the man pinioned beneath him.

"God, Draven, you feel so good," Taylor gasped, his voice husky. "Please, it's been too long. I need to feel you in me."

Draven laughed sharply, but he also felt the overwhelming desire to plunge his very needy cock into the hot, slick depths of his lover.

"You have been a cock tease all night and now it's my turn," he growled. "Licking your lips and touching yourself, and those damn toes of yours are about to get what they deserve."

His mouth found Taylor's, ravenous and greedy, and Draven got lost in the movement of Taylor's lips on his and the slick tongue that delved into the deepest recesses of Draven's willing mouth. Cocks rubbed together, legs twined like vines, as both men tried hard to absorb each other, feel each other and taste each other. Finally Draven lifted glazed eyes to gaze down into Taylor's, eyes blown and wide, lips swollen and wet from kisses.

"Keep your hands above your head," he demanded as he slowly worked his way down Taylor's body, worshipping the wriggling, panting man under his control. "You don't touch yourself or anything else. You're mine to do with what I want."

"But I need…" Taylor whined as his hands fisted the pillows and his hips arched up toward Draven's heated body. Draven bit the skin of his hip, the soft, smooth flesh like that of a ripe peach beneath his teeth. Taylor cried out sharply, his body bucking and Draven bit him again, softer this time, then licked the skin languorously.

"Behave," he said hoarsely, his own prick so hard that his groin was ready to blow. "I'm running the show. Lie back and enjoy."

Taylor moaned and the sound went straight to Draven's dick. He moved down the warm, spicy-scented skin, licking, nibbling, biting, loving the mewls and soft sobs as Taylor writhed on the bed. Finally he got where he wanted to be. He rubbed his stubbled cheek against a hardened, wet prick then licked the tip of it, rolling his tongue around the glans and finding that little hidden spot beneath.

"Oh God, Dray," Taylor said brokenly, "please, please. I need to come. Want you inside me."

Draven ignored him and instead, lifted Taylor's legs up toward his chest. He lost his breath at the sight of Taylor's dusky pucker, all ready for him, inviting him in. He reached up and spat on his fingers, then slowly rubbed that little hole and saw Taylor fall apart. His legs tensed, his hands forgetting they were supposed to be above his head and he tried to grab his already slippery cock. His groans were enough to make Draven erupt. He grasped the base of his prick desperately, willing it to last, then bent over Taylor, almost folding him in half. He put his hands back where they were supposed to be. "If you want me to fuck you," Draven whispered, "you'll know what's good for you. Don't move your hands again."

Taylor nodded, his eyes wild, his chest heaving and Draven gave him a deep, dirty kiss then went back to his teasing. Slowly, deliberately, he took Taylor's foot in his hand and sucked his toes into his mouth. He had no idea whether this was one of Taylor's erogenous zones but he wanted to find out. He wasn't disappointed. Taylor let out a howl at the first heavy suck of his toes, as Draven pulled them into his mouth, licking the firm flesh and sucking them with relish. They tasted earthy, spicy and uniquely Taylor. His fingers massaged the balls of Taylor's feet as he sucked and then he did the same to the other one. He thought with a sense of triumph that Taylor definitely had a thing for having his feet touched.

"Draven, oh fuck, Dray. Please, I need you to stop that, need you to fuck me. I'm begging you, please."

Draven didn't think he could last much longer himself. He reached for the lube and condom on the bedside table and in one of the quickest moves he'd ever made, the lube-covered condom was sheathing his cock and Taylor's hole was wet and slick as Draven rolled his fingers around that sensitive and pulsing area. Taylor was gripping the pillow above his head, eyes dark and wide, mouth pleading with Draven to hurry up.

"This isn't going to be one of those easy, tender, times, Tay," Draven warned as he pushed into Taylor. "This is going to be a rough ride. I need you too much. So damn much…"

He grunted as he filled the condom and Taylor, sinking into that little bit of heaven as if he belonged there. Taylor cried out, his muscles clenching around Draven as they found their rhythm and in between messy, sloppy kisses and murmured endearments, both men worked together as one.

It was about slick, hot flesh covered in lube and sweat, the sounds of sex echoing in the warm air, bodies pistoning and driving, arching and twisting and the feel of Taylor's hands on Draven's body, neither of them caring now about the old rule.

As Draven gasped and felt his balls constrict and as the first hot jets of fluid filled the condom and Taylor, he knew with absolute finality that this was where he belonged. With this man, in this man, and as part of this man and there was no way on God's green earth he was ever going to let him go.

His climax reached and spent, he heard Taylor's loud gasp of completion as his belly grew warm with Taylor's come and the scent of musk and sweat filled the air. Draven collapsed on the sticky, wet stomach of his lover. He sought Taylor's mouth and kissed him gently, not the rough, rude action born of desire or lust like before but rather the soft, passionate kiss of possession and affection.

"Mine," he whispered against Taylor's lips. "You are mine."

Taylor nodded, eyes sleepy. "Yours," he agreed. "Definitely."

Draven wanted to ask Taylor what had changed, why he'd been so forgiving and not given up on him, as they'd yet to speak about it. He didn't want to spoil the moment though, so instead he played big spoon to Taylor's little one, wrapping protective arms around the man in his arms, listening to his soft breathing as he fell asleep.

The feel of Taylor's warm arse against his groin and stomach made him feel complete.

Never felt like this before, must be something in the damn water, were his last thoughts before he drifted off into slumber.

*****

The following Sunday morning they sat in the lounge, eating marmalade toast and drinking coffee. Draven thought with a pang of longing that it was all very domesticated. He'd missed having this sort of relationship, the one where you woke up to the same man each morning and took pleasure in the way they liked the sugar in their coffee and saw the adorable frown as they perused the morning newspapers. He'd watched his mother and father as a child; seen their warmth and affection. He'd never really thought he'd want that, but since meeting Taylor it seemed to have become a need in his life. His job hadn't really allowed for it is the past, and he'd been too much of a player anyway but Taylor had put some things into perspective.

He grinned as Taylor's eyes travelled the newspaper, watched his lips part when he read something interesting, all the while taking bites of his toast which left crumbs on his mouth. His hair curled around his face, framing his smooth skin like a puddle of black ink.

Draven chuckled. "God, you look cute when you read the papers. Your nose scrunches up like a rabbit."

Taylor mock glared at him. "Comparing me to soft and cuddly animals isn't going to get you laid any time soon," he declared loftily. "I'd suggest you watch what you say."

"Yeah, yeah. You want this body far too badly to limit your partaking of it," Draven retorted, waving a hand languidly down his body. "You know you can't resist it."

Taylor stuck his tongue out at him and went back to reading his paper, a small smile on his face. Draven didn't want to disturb his well-being but there was no easy way and no good time to impart the information he had sitting in his head.

"Tay?"

Taylor looked up. "Hmm?"

"I spoke to Clay yesterday. It was the wife. She was the one in the room when Drew shot himself."

Taylor paled and he set the newspaper down on the table. "It was Catherine? But why, why didn't she stop him, what happened?"

Draven sat down next to Taylor and laid a warm hand on his. "While I was away, Clay went around to see her with one of his friends, some hotshot psychologist who knows just how to get under your skin. Believe me, I know. I've met her. Between them, they pushed Catherine into a place she'd never have known how to leave. They got the whole story. She was the one blackmailing him. She thought it might make him see the 'error of his ways' when it came to his alternative lifestyle." Draven grimaced in distaste. "She'd had enough of his antics and decided she wanted to teach him a lesson."

"She blackmailed her own husband?" Taylor looked ill. "What the fuck did she expect he'd do? Just sit back and let it ride?" He stood up and moved around the lounge in agitation. Draven watched him.

"She said she didn't mean for it to go so far. She'd had someone following him and they'd seen him go into the club. She had him take pictures and then used those to mess with his head.

"That night she got home early and found him in the study." Draven's voice tailed off. "Her story is he literally pulled the trigger as she saw him and she couldn't stop it. Clay said she was completely hysterical and they had to send for a paramedic to come and calm her down." He took a deep breath. "She's in some fancy sanatorium at the moment awaiting some doctor to tell the police whether anything further should be done. After all, she didn't pull the trigger."

Taylor's face was white. "No. But she drove him to it. If she hadn't been such a fucking bitch, he wouldn't be dead. How do you do that to someone you love, for God's sake? Blackmail them, drive them to suicide?" His hands were shaking, his breath laboured. Draven moved over to him quickly.

"Baby, breathe. Come on. Deep in, out, in, out…breathe for me, Taylor." He held his lover tight against his chest as the shudders lessened and then, when he was sure Taylor seemed better, he stepped back slightly and regarded him. "It's over, Tay. You helped Drew by getting the truth out. It won't change the fact he's dead but at least it's over now."

"It'll never be over. Not for me. I hear his death every time I close my eyes, see his blood coat those walls sometimes when I fall asleep. Nothing's ever over, Draven. Death isn't always the end."

Draven had no idea what to say to that, so he simply held Taylor close, feeling the beat of his heart against his own chest and the warmth that soaked into his skin from his boyfriend's body. Finally Taylor heaved a deep sigh. He looked up at Draven, his dark eyes shadowed.

"Sorry. That was probably a bit more intense that I meant to be. I just hope Drew's at peace wherever he is now. He deserved that much at least."

He moved over to the couch and slumped down, biting his fingernails. He looked a little lost and Draven couldn't stand it. He took a deep breath. "I'm going to the hospital this afternoon. Would you like to come with me to visit Jude?"

Taylor looked up him, face lightening "Are you sure?" he asked hesitantly. "Because I'd love to if you are."

Draven nodded, even as his heart beat faster. Jude's plight had been his cross to bear, for not being there to protect his brother, or make his world right and bring him back. He was trying to share because he knew if he didn't, he'd lose Taylor one day as well. "I think it's about time you met the other man in my life," he murmured. "So if we leave just after twelve, we won't be in the nurse's way at lunchtime and I won't have the smell of hospital food clogging my nostrils."

"Okay." Taylor looked uncertain. "Erm, I'm normally okay in hospitals, although I can tend to space out now and then if there's too much going on. I know I need some emotional connection to see stuff but hospitals are a bit of an unknown." He stood up and walked over to Draven, laying a hand on his shoulder. "So I'll try not to pass out on you or anything, but it might be a scenario we have to face."

Draven was mystified. "Then why the hell do you want to go in there, if it makes you uncomfortable?"

Taylor brushed warm lips across his. "Because it's something I want to share with you," he said simply. "It eats at you and I want to be there for you."

Draven's chest warmed and he pulled Taylor against him and hugged him fiercely. "Thanks," he said gruffly. "Just please try hold it together, though. I hate seeing you all whacked out." He released his lover and started clearing away the breakfast dishes. "Let me get rid of these and then I have some work to do in the study for a while. Can you entertain yourself while I'm gone?"

Taylor smirked. "You have a 48-inch TV, an X-Box and the latest *Grand Theft Auto*. I'm pretty sure I'll be fine."

*****

Draven felt strangely out of sorts later on that day as he entered the hospital lobby with Taylor. It was only the second time he'd been to the hospital to see Jude with someone. The first time had been with Clay. His boss had been with him when Draven had gotten the call telling him about the tragedy. If he hadn't been there, Draven knew he would have fallen apart. He remembered that call vividly, and he shivered now at remembering being told his whole family had just been ripped away from him.

Clay had been supportive but tenacious, like a dog humping his leg, until Draven gave in and took him to visit Jude at the hospital. From that point on, Jude had two frequent visitors. Draven knew that Clay had some personal issues of his own in the mysterious man that took up a lot of his time, but he'd always managed to pay a visit to the young man lying prone in a hospital bed.

Draven turned to look at Taylor, who followed behind him. Taylor had seemed hesitant to enter the hospital and Draven wondered if he was feeling any vibes or having visions. He cocked an eyebrow at his boyfriend. "Are you okay? You've been very quiet on the way over here."

In truth, Taylor had hardly said a word. It was as if he'd been psychically building himself up to be here, in the slight movement of his lips, the deep breathing and the nervous twitching of his fingers as he picked at the seam on his worn jeans. He'd smoked numerous cigarettes earlier on in the garden and then glared at the packet in disgust afterward and said he was giving up. The packet had been thrown unceremoniously in the garbage bin and Draven wondered just how long Taylor would hold out.

Taylor gave a faint smile. "I'm all right. I just don't like hospitals much. Reminds me of when my mum died." He seemed to anticipate Draven's heated response of "You didn't have to come if it upset you" with a wave of his hand. "Before you go all postal on me, I want to be here. And no, I'm not tuned in to anything at the moment, so you don't need to worry." He frowned slightly. "Although there's something not quite right, but I can't really put my finger on it. It's as if it's there but not there, if you know what I mean."

Draven stared at him. He had no idea at all what that meant. Sometimes his lover said the weirdest things. He nodded absently. "Uh-huh. Come on. Let's do this then."

Five minutes later he was standing outside Jude's partially open door, his chest tight as he took a deep breath.

Taylor rubbed his back gently. "I'm here with you," he said simply. "Come on." He pushed Draven softly into the room. Draven saw Sister Alison fiddling with the transparent lines leading into Jude's body and she gave a wide, white smile when she saw Draven.

"Draven. Lovely to see you, sweetie. Jude, your brother's here, honey. And he's brought a very tasty young man with him." She

grinned at Draven, winking at him and giving him a secret thumbs
up. "Now we know who's been keeping your brother company." Her
brows furrowed as she looked behind Draven.

Draven smiled and reached out and touched his brother's cheek.
It was warmer than usual and he caressed the pale skin. "Hi little bro,
I bought someone to meet you." He turned to introduce Taylor and
his heart almost stuttered to a stop. Taylor was white, his hands held
loosely at his sides, his eyes blank. He resembled a wax mannequin
at Madam Tussauds.

Draven wasn't even sure he could see the rise and fall of
Taylor's chest.

"Taylor?" He swiftly moved to Taylor's side and touched his
arm. "What's wrong?"

Alison was beside him now, her face racked in concern. She
stared at Draven in confusion. "Is he all right? I saw him behind you
when you came in and he…just…well, he just stopped dead."

A feeling of dread assailed Draven. "Alison, I can't really
explain, but he has these turns now and then. I'll get him sat down,
and I'm sure he'll be okay in a minute. Can I ask you to get him a
Coke or something? Sometimes his blood sugar gets a bit low…"
His voice trailed off and he knew Alison wasn't buying the story,
nurse as she was. Her eyes narrowed but to his relief she simply
nodded.

"Yes, I'll get him something. You get him settled there in that
easy chair. I'll be back in a little while."

The sister left the room and Draven took hold of Taylor's
unresisting body. "Come and sit down, Tay." He managed to get his
lover seated in the chair as Taylor's eyes still gazed unseeingly into
the distance. It was as if there was no one home, just the shell of a
body left in the wake of whatever had lived in there before. Draven's
spine prickled with fear.

"Taylor, please, baby. Where the hell are you?" He ran a hand
through his hair, leaving it messy and rumpled. "I knew this was a
bad idea to bring you into a hospital with dying and sick people. I
just knew it…" He continued to stare helplessly at the man in the
chair, as he sat down next to him in another seat and placed one hand
on his thigh, and the other on Jude's hand in the bed. His hands
trembled.

Hopefully both of the men in my life can feel me and know I'm here for them. Christ, what the hell do I do now?

*****

Taylor was aware of Draven beside him, aware of the fear and panic on his face but he was powerless to do or say anything. Instead, all he could do was gaze in wonder into the dark, azure blue of *somewhere*, God knew where, as a slight and blond figure stood outlined against the backdrop of deep blue, rich and vibrant colour that assailed Taylor's vision like a starlit night.

"Hello, Taylor," Jude said as he stepped forward. "I've been waiting for you."

"How…how is this possible?" Taylor croaked, his voice dry with both awe and fear. "Where are we?"

Jude's slim shoulders shrugged. "We call it Earthlight. It's a kind of in-between place, it's the only way I can describe it."

Taylor gazed around him in wonder. "Maybe I should have asked *what* it is?"

Dark grey eyes exactly like Draven's stared at him. The young man looked to be in his early teens and Taylor knew Jude had been fifteen going on sixteen when he'd had his car accident. He was almost a carbon copy of a young Draven, although much slimmer built.

"It's just a place people like me come to. People who can't move on, because something is holding them back. It's a sort of holding pen, I suppose." He smiled and Taylor saw Draven in that soft lift of the lips. His eyes strayed toward his brother with a glance of affection. Taylor followed them and saw Draven sitting, eyes closed, a look of defeat on his face, as he talked to someone, probably trying to bring Taylor back. Taylor's heart clenched at the look of sadness he wore.

"My brother loves me, I know that," Jude said quietly. "He feels guilty that he was the only one who lived, and he feels he should have been the one to die instead of me and Mum and Dad." His face was anguished. "He tells me this when he visits and I want to reach out and tell him he's wrong, he needs to live his life and stop beating himself up over everything. But I can't." Taylor heard the desperation in his tone. "You have to help him and me, Taylor. You need to tell him to let me go so both of us can move on." His eyes observed the machines and the fluids keeping him alive. "I've come to terms with the fact I'm dead. He needs to do that now too."

Taylor shook his head. "It will destroy him," he said quietly. "I can't tell him what he should do."

"No, you can't," Jude said. "But *I* can. It's my life, whatever that may mean," he snorted grimly, "and I want to leave here and be with my folks. I've heard him talk about you, and what you can do and I knew the only way I could get through to him was through you. I've waited so long to see you. I tried reaching out to you but it just wasn't enough. His grief and his guilt blocked me and I wasn't strong enough to get through to you being so far away."

His voice dropped. "I'm tired, Taylor," he whispered. "Tired of being in a halfway house kept alive by machinery. It's comfortable enough, here, I suppose, and I'm not alone but I miss my parents." His voice shook. "They're waiting for me to move on, but I can't. I love my brother dearly, but he needs to let go of me. Only you can make him see that's what he has to do."

Taylor's eyes were burning, filling with bitter tears. "I don't think he'll listen," he murmured, his throat closing up with the lump in it. "He loves you so much, Jude."

Jude smiled sadly. "You know there's that old cheesy saying about if you love someone, let them go? Speak to Draven for me. You're the only one who can. My brother loves you, you know. He might have a tough time showing you or believing it himself sometimes, but he does. I can hear it in his voice when he says your name." His eyes glistened with tears.

"Tell him he can take comfort that there is another side to life and one day, he'll be here with us. It's not goodbye, just *au revoir*." He grinned faintly. "If he needs any convincing that you've spoken to me and you weren't hallucinating, tell him this." He hesitated then spoke softly. "'Our brothers and sisters are there with us from the dawn of our personal stories to the inevitable dusk.' It's a quote made by an author called Susan Scarf Merrell. He enjoyed reading her books and he was really drawn to this quote. He used to say it to me all the time. Remind him I'll always be there for him. Tell him I love him." His face softened. "And tell him Pudsey says hello."

Jude's voice and figure grew fainter. Taylor blinked past the tears in his eyes, both from the fact Jude was in pain and the fact that he believed Draven loved him, and watched the form shimmer. His head swum, his skin prickled and then as the last vestiges of deep blue and Jude faded away, he closed his eyes and fell into darkness.

Chapter 10

There isn't really a Hallmark greeting card to advise a current boyfriend that his comatose younger brother has been in contact with your psychic other half and requested that his life support system be switched off.

Taylor wished there was.

It would make talking to Draven *so* much easier. Even as he knew the complete incongruity and craziness of this thought, he was thinking how best to approach the subject with the man who now sat broodingly beside him in the car, hands clenched on the wheel, a look of ferocious calm on his bruised face.

It was Taylor's fault that his lover looked as damaged as he did. In coming around from his zone-out, Taylor had flailed so wildly that he'd ended up hitting Draven in the face. He now sported a rather nasty-looking bruise under his eye, which no doubt was going to turn black.

Looking at the silent man beside him, then at the dark grey rain outside, Taylor knew that Draven's current taciturnity had been fear over the fact that once again Taylor had zoned out. The look of helplessness in those slate grey eyes as he'd stared at Taylor doing the crazy chicken dance with thrashing limbs had been sobering.

Afterwards, Draven had made like the proverbial bad-tempered bear and growled that he was "damn sick of all this shit." He'd said his goodbyes to Jude and stormed off to the car, Taylor stumbling unsteadily behind him. As they drove back toward Draven's house, thoughts circled in Taylor's head like hungry sharks all waiting to get a piece of him.

"I'm sorry I hit you," he muttered quietly. "When we get to your place, you should put some ice on that eye. Maybe even some arnica ointment if you have some. If you don't, I'll walk down to that corner chemist and get you some. That always helped me, my mum used to swear by it…"

"Taylor, it's fine." Draven sounded tired but his earlier ire seemed to have dissipated. "Don't worry. You couldn't help yourself." His one hand left the steering wheel and he gingerly touched the swelling under his eye. "It's not my first black eye, you know."

"Yes, but it's the first one from me," Taylor grumbled.

Draven snorted softly and Taylor was relieved to see the corners of his mouth lift up. "I hope that isn't saying there might be more to come?"

Taylor reached over and shoved his arm half-heartedly. "I bloody well hope there aren't."

Draven smiled, but it didn't reach his eyes. He concentrated on driving through the gentle drizzle, squinting slightly. Taylor knew he must have questions.

"Don't you want to know what happened back there?" he asked softly.

Draven shook his head, lips pressed together. "Not now. I can't talk about that shit and focus on getting home safely. I hate driving in the rain. So I'd rather you not tell me now. When we get back to my place…" he heaved a deep sigh. "Maybe then." He glanced at Taylor, almost nervously but said nothing more. Taylor nodded and leaned back against the headrest, shutting his eyes. The next thing he knew he was being shaken awake.

"Tay? We're home. Come on. It's pouring fucking cats and dogs now. I need a drink."

Taylor nodded sleepily and clambered out of the car, following Draven as he dashed for the front door. Once inside, Draven disappeared into the kitchen as Taylor shook the wet from his hair and grimaced.

"Uggh. I wasn't made for wet weather. I should be somewhere warm and dry, where the sun shines all day and I can work on a tan. This shitty weather is not for me."

Draven came through bearing two large glasses of red wine. He handed one to Taylor. "You and me both. I'm not crazy about sun-tanning; I burn too easily but you…" He appraised Taylor. "You're dark enough with that skin tone. Works for me anyway. I like you just the way you are." He padded through to the lounge in stocking feet and plonked himself down in an easy chair.

Taylor followed, feeling a warmth at Draven's words. He divested himself of his boots and jacket as he did. "Just the way I am, hey? Perhaps less clothes?" He waggled his eyebrows cheekily, bringing a reluctant grin to Draven's pale face. The bruise around his eye was beginning to darken and Taylor felt guilty at being the cause.

"That'll work too. Maybe later. Right now you need to tell me what the hell went down in that hospital room." Draven's eyes searched Taylor's face as he fell, loose limbed, onto the couch, and draped his feet over the end of the arm. He took a slurp of his drink and then placed the glass on the side table. Draven watched him unwaveringly as he sipped his wine.

Taylor cleared his throat. "You need to listen to me, okay? This isn't going to be easy. Hell, it took me by surprise and I've lived with this sort of thing all my life. I need you to be open minded and not fly off at the deep end—"

Draven interrupted him impatiently. "Taylor, just tell me, blabbermouth. I'm sure I can cope with whatever it is. I'm a big boy."

Despite the confident words, Taylor heard the fear. He tried to inject some levity in the hope it might soothe Draven. "I know that; hell, I've had you up my arse, so I'm very personally acquainted with how big you are."

"Tay," Draven growled.

Taylor sighed. "Fine. There isn't an easy way to say this so I'm just going to say it." He took a deep breath. "I saw Jude. He's in some in-between place and he really wants to move on, to be with your folks. He told me to ask you to please let him go. He wants you to switch off the life support."

Draven's face whitened and the stem of his wineglass shattered in his fingers. The bulb of the glass fell to the floor, causing what looked a pool of blood to land on the pale carpet. Taylor sat up and stared at the fluid dripping from Draven's fingers.

"Dray, you're bleeding. Here, let me get a cloth." He started to rise from the couch but Draven stood up in one cat like movement and pushed him back onto the couch.

"Sit the fuck down." He prodded Taylor in the chest with one hard finger, and Taylor watched, mesmerised, as small globules of blood landed on his Iron Maiden tee shirt. "What the hell do you mean, you saw Jude? I thought you said you didn't see dead people?"

Draven's face was thunderous, his eyes glinting with both suppressed anger and what looked a lot to Taylor like sheer panic. He looked up at Draven, trying to figure out what to say next without causing further injury to what was already a frightened and hurting soul.

"I don't normally, so I can't explain it. Maybe it's because Jude is in this place between living and dead, I don't know. I've never come across this before. But it was him, Draven. I talked to him."

The prodding stopped and Draven stood back, his body taut. "The fuck you say. My little brother wants me to kill him?"

Taylor held Draven's gaze. "He's already dead, Draven," he said steadily, swallowing the bile in his throat. "The machines keep him alive, nothing else. He's come to terms with that and wants you to do the same."

Draven stalked like a caged tiger around the room. He stopped and pointed a finger at Taylor. "He's all I have left in the world, and you want me to stop what's keeping him alive?"

Taylor's heart ached at the words that Jude was all Draven had but he knew the man was shocked. "It's not what *I* want, Draven. This isn't about me."

Draven laughed harshly. "How am I supposed to deal with this? It's all getting too damn much. Sometimes I wish I'd never met you, that I didn't know you talk to dead people and tell people things they don't want to hear."

Taylor swallowed. "I'm sorry you feel that way." His throat was dry, his stomach roiling at Draven's harsh words. "I'm just a messenger, believe me, it's no fucking fun for me either. I didn't ask for this gift, I was cursed with it, and sometimes it seems more heartache than it's worth."

"I don't need this shit," Draven spat. "I don't need to know my comatose brother is talking to my lover and telling him he needs to die to be happy. I just…"

His voice tailed off and Taylor's heart ached at the bleak look on Draven's face.

"I'm sorry," he said helplessly as he stood up and moved toward Draven, hoping to touch him, comfort him. "I can only tell you what I see and hear."

"Well, I didn't fucking ask for it!" Draven snarled.

Taylor's temper flared. "I'm sorry that I'm not able to switch it on and off like a fucking light switch, Dray, just to stop you hurting. I'm just passing on a message from a boy that thinks you're holding onto him for your own needs, not his."

The words echoed in the air and Taylor wished he hadn't said them. Draven's hand rose like a blur toward his face and he closed his eyes, waiting for the slap or the punch that he thought was coming. When nothing happened, he opened his eyes to see Draven staring at him then at his upraised hand with haunted eyes. The desolation on his face wrenched at Taylor's chest.

"I was going to hit you," Draven whispered, his voice agonised. "Christ, I was going to bloody slap you."

"But you didn't," Taylor said, his voice shaking. "You stopped. So it doesn't count."

Draven's face was bleak. "It counts to me. Intent is as good as doing it."

Taylor shook his head vehemently. "Don't talk such crap. It's the action that counts. We all have impulses, which bring out our bad side. It's not acting on them that makes us the better man."

Draven turned and strode over to the front door. He opened it and beckoned Taylor over. "You need to leave."

Taylor stared at him. "Leave? Draven, this isn't going to go away when I do. I *spoke* to Jude. He asked me to tell you to let him move on. He even quoted some damn line from a book from some author, Susan Scart Milly someone or other, about brothers and sisters. He said it was your favourite quote."

Draven's eyes flinched at that, as if recognising the quote, and Taylor took hope and pressed on. "He wants to be with your folks, wants to be at peace. You can't deny him that."

"Leave." Draven's tone was uncompromising, his shoulders ramrod straight, his face unrelenting. "I should never have gotten involved with you. All you do is confuse people with your bloody so-called psychic crap and I want no more part of it. "

Taylor's heart broke and his eyes prickled with tears. "Honestly? That's your answer to all this, to bury your damn head in the sand and push everyone away who gets close to you?" He shook his head. "I'm just the messenger, Draven. I always have been. I can't distort the truth or tell lies, and I thought you'd realised that. Obviously I was wrong."

Eyes blinded with hot tears, he fumbled for his shoes and slid his feet into them. "Fine. You want me gone, I'll go. But I'm warning you. Don't call me again with apologies until you've got your head right." He shrugged into his jacket and fastened it with shaking hands. Draven still stood as still as someone frozen in time in an old film clip.

Taylor tried to calm his racing heart, and the sobs that threatened to well up. It had been an emotional day and he hated himself for feeling so vulnerable.

He walked to the still-opened door and as he reached the step outside, he turned back to look at Draven, whose face was set, his lips pinched.

"I'm going to say this once, so listen. I know I shouldn't have but I really care for you." Taylor swallowed as the lump in his throat grew bigger and his chest grew tighter. "I know it's only been a short while but I thought we had something starting. It looks like it's one-sided.

"In case we don't see each other again, I thought you should know. Perhaps one day when you sit down and think about everything I've told you, you'll realise I never meant to hurt you, I just wanted to help." Tears were rolling down his cheeks now. "I hope you think about things, Dray. For your and Jude's sake."

Draven continued to stare at him through eyes that seemed carved out of obsidian.

Taylor tried to smile but wasn't sure he'd pulled it off. "Jude told me something else. He said to tell you Pudsey said hello. I hope whatever or whoever that is, it brings you comfort. Goodbye, Draven."

Taylor turned away and walked down the stone steps to the pavement and didn't take another glance backward. His eyes were so filled with hot tears it was unlikely he'd have seen anything anyway. He wanted to get home to his place, to Leslie, who would cuddle and mother him, make him feel loved and wrap him in blankets and hold him tight. Then he wanted to fall into darkness and sleep the pain away.

*****

Draven closed the door behind Taylor's departing figure and moved to the kitchen. He was numb, confused, his chest ached with pain he'd never experienced before and his hand hurt like shit from where he'd cut it. Drops of blood spattered the carpet in neat lines, and he ignored that as he reached the kitchen sink and washed away the blood that caked his fingers. Like an automaton, he pulled out the first aid box from the cupboard under the sink, put plaster on the cut then took a bottle of carpet cleaner and a rag back into the lounge and hallway to try to repair the damage he'd done on the carpet. For some minutes he busied himself with cleaning up the mess, scrubbing the blood away and trying to forget the past few hours had ever happened.

Finally, he dropped the blood-soaked cloth in the laundry basket then stood stock still in the kitchen as his stomach tensed and his hands shook. With eyes as gritty as a beach full of sand, he took deep breaths to stave off the panic that threatened as random thoughts flooded his brain.

Dear God, I nearly hit Taylor.

I told him to leave, that I didn't want him. I hurt him so badly. Those tears, God, he looked shattered. He said he cares for me. Does he love me? If he did, he probably doesn't anymore.

Hell, I love him so damn much.

Fuck, my comatose brother wants me to switch off his life support and let him go.

"What the fuck kind of karma is this then?" Draven shouted into the empty kitchen. His hands clenched at his sides. "Have I been such an arsehole in a past life that I get to make these kinds of decisions? I didn't fucking ask for this."

He sank to his knees on the kitchen floor, head bowed as tears overcame him. The sense of loss at Taylor's departure; the keen agony of knowing that he'd been telling the truth when he said he'd spoken to Jude; the fact he'd actually raised his hand to Taylor in his pain—all this came surging into his head and he swore loudly, profanity echoing in the still kitchen.

"Fuck you, Jude, fuck you, Taylor and fuck you, Draven bloody Samuels for your pig headedness."

The outburst didn't make him feel any better. He moved and sat back against the kitchen cupboard, arms wrapped about his body, trying to make sense of it all. When he finally looked up, the accusing eyes of Freud, the cookie jar, on the counter opposite him seemed to stare right into his soul. Draven stared at the overly large eyes of the pig and whispered to it brokenly.

"I didn't mean to send Taylor away. I think I just panicked. He knew the quote, the one Jude and I used to say to each other. No one alive knows that. It was our secret quote." He sniffed and wiped his running nose with his shirt sleeve.

"And he knew about Pudsey. Only Jude could have told him about that stupid cat; I've never mentioned him." He smiled through his tears as he gazed into what now looked like the eyes of a more sympathetic pig.

"We found Pudsey in the shed, all mauled and broken. We fixed him up and stole food and stuff from the kitchen because Mum didn't like cats. When he was better, Jude snuck him into his room. I told him if Mum and Dad found him, they'd make him get rid of him, but he was adamant. So we kept him hidden for about three weeks until we came down to the kitchen one night looking for midnight snacks and found our folks waiting for us.

"They'd known about the damn cat for weeks and were waiting for us to come clean." Draven laughed sadly. "They gave us a real bollocking but when it came down to it, they let us keep him. He died of old age years ago."

Freud looked on wisely, a beneficent smile on his ceramic face. He didn't seem too worried about the demise of the cat and Draven scowled.

"He was a damn good cat so take that look off your face." He groaned. "Dear heavens, I'm talking to a damn cookie jar again. I'm really losing my mind. Taylor would laugh himself silly at that."

His voice tailed off as he realised he probably had no Taylor anymore. He struggled to his feet and picked up his phone, cold tendrils of fear winding themselves through his skin and up his spine. "I fucked up, Freud. Big-time. I need to call him, tell him to come back. Do you think he'll listen to me? God, I can't lose Taylor too. I love him, even if I can't tell him that yet."

He dialled Taylor's number and listened anxiously at the ring tone. No one picked up and finally it went to Taylor's voice mail.

Hi, you've reached Taylor. Leave me a message and I'll get back to you.

"Taylor, it's me. I, uhmm, I'm sorry, I was upset and I took it out on you. Again. Please call me, Tay. I'm so damned fucked up I'm talking to my cookie jar and believe me, that pig isn't a great conversationalist. I know you were telling the truth. I believe in you. You said you cared about me, and that's," his voice choked, "That's good to know." He winced as he said those words.

Good to know? Way to go, Draven.

"Anyway, call me back when you get this message. I have something to tell you too. In person. Bye."

He put his mobile down on the kitchen top and glanced at Freud. The pig stared back.

"I can't do this without him," Draven murmured. "I can't help Jude the way he wants me to if Taylor isn't with me. I need him. I'm not strong enough. Not on my own."

He left the kitchen and went to the hall cupboard. He pulled out an old blanket and went back into the lounge. There, he switched on the television for background noise and settled himself on the couch, mobile beside him. He wanted to be able to answer his phone straight away if Taylor rang back.

Draping the blanket over his chilled body, Draven sat and watched the rain pummel down outside and run down the windowpanes like escaping sperm. He tried not to think about what the future held.

He called Clay, needing to hear a familiar voice. If he'd thought that Clay would be sympathetic to his plight, he was wrong.

"Shit, Draven, you what?" Clay exclaimed. "Christ, are all your brains in your dick and when you come, you lose them? You and I both know that man is the best thing that ever happened to you. We've talked about it often enough."

Draven curled his fingers in both anger and guilt. "I called him to apologise and he's not picking up," he growled. "What am I supposed to do? Kidnap the guy and hold him prisoner until he gives in?"

There was silence on the other end of the phone. Then Clay sighed. "I guess it doesn't work for everyone," he muttered and Draven's jaw dropped.

"What? You mean you've actually done that? I was bloody kidding, you psycho."

"What? Oh. Of course." Clay's voice sounded hesitant, unusually so for a man who had a rod of steel in his back and the balls and principles to match. "I was joking too."

Draven wasn't quite so sure but he didn't push it. There was time enough to find out more about that cryptic statement later. Right now, he had a man to win back.

Clay continued. "Well, all I can say is keep wearing him down and hope he'll come around. I mean, he's right, Dray. If that's what Jude wants, maybe you need to listen."

Draven shook his head in wonderment. "You believe him when he says he talked to my brother? I thought this whole thing might have been a bridge too far even for you. I never thought I'd see the day when solid, earth-based Clay Mortimer fell into the hole that is Alice in Wonderland and believes someone actually speaks to people on another plane of existence."

Clay sounded sad when he next spoke. "Not everything can be explained in science. If you'd read the reports from some of the people Taylor has helped with his gift, and when you've been where I have trying to stop someone you love going the opposite way and killing them…" He stopped, seeming aware that he'd revealed too much. "Anyway, I have an open mind. You need to keep one too. For both your and Jude's sake. I love that boy, Draven. But if he's suffering or wants to move on, I rather think that's his prerogative, don't you?"

"I thought you said you tried to stop someone killing themselves," Draven remarked quietly, reading between the lines not written. "Isn't that their choice too?"

"No you fucker, it is not." Clay growled. "This person is alive, walking around and in possession of all their faculties. They need help. Your brother is not one of those people, no matter how you want to sugar coat it.

"I can't tell you what to do about Jude, Dray. But I can tell you that you need to work on getting Taylor back if you love him. Don't let him go." There was an element of pain in Clay's voice and Draven very much wanted to pry, but he knew Clay. The man wouldn't spill his guts without extreme pressure and now was not the time.

So he thanked his friend, mentor and boss for his advice and went back to staring at the pig.

Chapter 11

Four days later and Draven was going out of his mind. Taylor still hadn't called back. It was a grim reminder of the last time Draven had been an arsehole, only this time, he wasn't so sure that it was going to be fixed. His texts and calls were going unanswered. Draven knew there was only one thing he could do. Face the dragons in their den and call on some support that hopefully wouldn't punch him in the face.

It was why he found himself in Galileo's that evening, hopping from foot to foot in anxiety and apprehension by the reception desk, as he waited for Eddie Tripp to make his appearance.

Gideon had been sympathetic to his plight but told him in no uncertain terms that Eddie was pretty mad with him and he'd better watch his right hook. Then he arranged for his boyfriend to take time out from the kitchen to meet with Draven. There was added fuel to the best friend fire, apparently, as Leslie, too, was at the restaurant on a blind date. Draven hoped fervently that he didn't have to face them both down. He didn't think he'd survive it.

Alas, his hopes were dashed when he saw the pair striding toward him, one whose piercing green eyes were fixed firmly on his face with an expression of murder, the other dressed to kill in a simple but elegant suit worn with stiletto heels.

Draven blinked as the Avenging Furies made their way toward him. He was a man who dealt with corporate spies, bad men and all manner of crazy and dangerous people, but the two best friends of the man he loved were making him wet his pants. He took a deep breath and told himself to man up.

In the distance, he saw Gideon smoothly intercept them both, laying a firm hand on Eddie's shoulder until some of the tenseness disappeared. He gave his lover a soft kiss and then waved them on their way with a wicked stare at Draven. Draven's insides quailed as he came face to face with hostility—and in Leslie's case, a man bag held in such a way that it looked as if it was about to meet Draven's head.

He gulped. "Evening, Eddie. Leslie. Thanks for seeing me."

Eddie's eyes glinted. "Thank Gideon. If it was up to me I'd be sticking my size eleven up your arse."

Draven's eyebrows lifted. He blamed the next sentence on the fact he was nervous. "Size eleven, hey? Gideon must be pleased…" His voice tailed off at the shift of Eddie's body closer to him. "I mean, thanks. For not sticking your shoes up my backside."

"The evening is still young." Leslie's modulated tones belied the look of violence in his eyes. "I'd say size eleven followed by a size ten." He waggled a high-heeled shoe on the bottom of a very shapely ankle at Draven, who winced.

Gideon appeared like a wraith at Draven's side, seeming to be barely holding back a grin. "Now come on, guys. Play nice. Draven here is eating humble pie and having the courage to come and face you two. I can't say I'd do the same in his shoes. I know you both better. Eddie, babe, give the man a break. Leslie, my little barracuda, stop scaring the man. Hear Draven out." He pressed Draven's shoulder in a comforting gesture. "I have a kitchen to be in. I suggest you use my office for a bit of privacy. Good luck." Gideon grinned and left them alone.

Leslie sniffed. "Office sounds good. Come on, follow me."

He sashayed off, Eddie and Draven following behind him. Soon they were safely ensconced in an office that smelt of sweat and cologne, and Draven was sure he smelt sex odours. He wasn't about to say anything though.

"Soooo," Leslie chirped, his dark blue eyes narrowed. "You said you needed our help. Why should we help you when you've done nothing but hurt Taylor? He's a complete damn wreck at the moment."

There was a noise behind the slightly opened connecting door to what looked like a storage room on the far side of the office. Eddie's eyes darted in its direction before coming back to rest on Draven, as he crossed his arms across a tight, muscled chest and scowled.

Draven had a speech all prepared on how they could perhaps convince his ex-lover that he was sorry, that they should meet face to face and that he'd been a prick and needed to see him, but seeing the concern and affection on their faces for their friend left him speechless. Instead, he went with his heart.

"You shouldn't really. I mean, I'm a tough guy to like, but he said he cared about me and that's all I've got left. I've got something difficult to do at the hospital, and the only way I think I can face it is with Taylor by my side." He swallowed. "I was a bastard and I told him to leave, but I didn't mean it because, Christ, I really want the guy in my life and I don't know what I'd do if he never came back."

Eddie's scowl lessened. "We heard about your brother. Sorry, but we dragged the whole story out of Taylor. He needed to talk about it." His tone softened. "I'm sorry you have to go through that with a family member. I have no idea how that feels. It's a really tough decision to make and I wouldn't wish it on anyone."

Leslie nodded. "I can't even imagine how I'd feel. I have two sisters and an older brother and I'd hate to be in that situation. That's why we said we'd speak to you. Extenuating circumstances and all that crap." He waved a slim, pale hand. "Anyhoo, back to Tay."

He moved closer to Draven, his full-lipped pink mouth coming so close Draven had a sudden panic he was about to be kissed. Not that it would be hardship because Leslie was damn sexy with his pouty lips and black bangs, but Draven had only one man's mouth in mind when he thought of kissing the hell out of someone, and it wasn't Leslie. Instead, Leslie invaded his personal space and leaned in to whisper in Draven's ear.

"You need to really tell him how you feel, right now. He needs to hear it." Then Leslie moved away. Draven stared at him in confusion.

"I just told you how I feel about him."

Leslie just faked a yawn and cast a meaningful glance toward the open door. Eddie was smiling softly and all of a sudden Draven thought he knew what was going on. His heart filled with hope and he nodded slowly.

"I'm not very good with words, more of an action man," he ignored Leslie's snort, "but I'll try." His throat was dry and he watched as Leslie and Eddie quietly exited the office with a nod of approval his way. Draven walked over and locked the door. He knew he'd only get one chance to do this right.

"I sat at home talking to Freud, my pig and realised something. That pig isn't much of a talker but he's a good listener. I told him how much I cared about a certain person, and that I'd driven him away. I told him how I'd fucked up and I'd do anything to get him back because I didn't think I could make it without him."

He walked quietly to the door and hesitated. Taking a deep breath, he pushed the door open to reveal Taylor standing behind it, surrounded by towels and napkins stacked neatly on shelves. His eyes widened as Draven came closer. He looked tired, his eyes rimmed with dark circles and his usual coffee-coloured skin paler than usual.

He was wearing one of Draven's old hoodies, with the words "Live and Let Live" written across it. It had been one Draven had lent him when they'd been caught in the rain one day and Taylor had needed something warm. Of course, the subsequent undressing and pulling off wet clothes had led to hot sex in the shower and it was a memory Draven cherished.

Draven's heart stuttered in his chest at the thought Taylor still wore his clothes. "I said to Freud that I needed him. Like I need breath in my body to live, like water to a man dying of thirst."

Taylor's eyes flickered and his breath hitched. His fingers were fidgeting at his sides as his dark eyes watched Draven move closer.

"And do you know what that damn pig said to me? He said to me, 'Draven, you're an idiot and if you don't go after that man and convince him that you want him, that you need him, then you'll have lost something precious.' So I decided that's exactly what I'd do."

Draven stood as close as he could to Taylor, closing his eyes to the warm male body heat emanating from him. He opened them to see the rise and fall of his chest and the widening of his eyes as Draven reached out and gently drew his fingers along lips he wanted so badly to kiss.

So he did. He pulled Taylor out of the storage room and into the office, gripping hips that were familiar to him.

His lips brushed Taylor's, softly at first then more possessively as Taylor sighed. Draven's tongue flicked across Taylor's mouth, willing him to open and let him in. When Taylor's lips parted and his arms wrapped around Draven's neck to pull him closer and he ground his hips against Draven's own hardness, Draven wanted to weep with relief. It was like coming home to a warm hearth, to a familiar place where you could be safe and happy.

That place was Taylor Abelard.

Taylor was murmuring something under his breath, words that sounded like "stupid bastard" and "look what you've been missing," and then his words were totally swallowed up as Draven took his mouth completely and tried to consume him.

Finally, they drew apart, panting and dishevelled, and Draven pulled Taylor into a hug that left no doubt as to his desire and need for him.

"I'm sorry," he whispered into Taylor's ear. "I'll spend the rest of my life making it up to you if you'll let me, but please, please don't let me alone again like this past week. It just wasn't the same waking up without you beside me."

Taylor chuckled softly. "You can be quite the poet, you know that? I never thought I'd hear the rough, macho Draven Samuels talking so sweet." He frowned. "There is one thing I need to know though."

"Name it," said Draven as he nuzzled Taylor's neck, breathing in his man's scent and tracing a path of wet down the side of his neck with his tongue.

"What the hell is it with you and this pig? I mean, am I going to be the piggy in the middle in this relationship or what, because getting between a man and his pig can be really serious—" His words were cut off by Draven's mouth taking possession of his once again plus the fact that Draven has just slid his hands into Taylor's sweatpants and palmed a very hardened cock.

"Oh, God," Taylor moaned as Draven closed his hand around it and began sliding his fingers along the slick shaft. "That feels, unggh, I missed your hands on me. Don't stop, or I might have to tell Freud you don't follow through on your promises…."

Draven chuckled as he slid another hand around to Taylor's arse to slide it over the firm cheeks and into his crack, meandering down to his hole. He slid his finger gently across the pucker, causing Taylor to buck in his arms and his cock to push into Draven's hand.

"Shhh. Forget the damn pig. Just enjoy yourself. I'm going to make you come so hard your balls will think they've exploded."

Taylor groaned, his hands reaching down into Draven's pants. Draven pushed them away. As much as he wanted to feel Taylor's hands on him, this wasn't *for* him. This was for Taylor.

"I'm fine, honey, just close your eyes and concentrate on me jacking you off. Focus on me doing this." He slid one finger inside Taylor, loving the moan that came out of his mouth and catching it with his lips. Taylor vibrated against him like a tuning fork and his breathy pants soon turned into gasps as his hips shuddered and hands clenched Draven anywhere they could find a grasp.

"Fuck, Draven, it's been too long. Oh sweet hell…" He warbled as Draven thrust yet another finger inside him, fucking him hard and deep. "That's it, I'm done." Warm fluid spurted over Draven's fingers and palm as Taylor's hole clenched around his fingers and his body shivered and quivered like a man being Tasered.

Draven held him close, breathing in the smell of sex and Taylor and wanting nothing more than this moment to last much longer.

Finally a small voice spoke up from where it nestled against Draven's shoulder. "I think the pig would approve."

Draven laughed out loud. He felt as if he'd been sleeping and just woken up from a dark dream. He leaned back and tucked Taylor's spent cock back into his underwear and arranged his sweatpants to be decent. His own hard-on clamoured for attention, but he thought that perhaps later he might be lucky enough to manage that situation with the help of the man now standing loose limbed before him, eyes softened and lips swollen.

Draven leaned his forehead against Taylor's as he brushed sweaty locks of black hair away from his cheeks. "I don't deserve you, but I'll work on it."

Taylor reached up and framed his face in hands that shook slightly. "I won't argue with that, you stubborn bastard. However, I'm no angel either and we're going to have to work at this thing." His face grew serious. "What I can't have is you chucking me out every time you get angry. I don't think I've got it in me to forgive you again." His eyes were solemn, his face earnest.

Draven nodded. "Fair enough. I don't think I've got it in me to face Eddie and Leslie one more time. I truly think they might hurt me if I go off the rails again. Those mates of yours are a great deterrent."

Taylor grinned smugly. "They're like Rottweilers that I let out when I need someone to be hunted down. They know how to maim and leave no evidence, so beware." He looked down at Draven's groin and licked his lips suggestively. "That looks painful. Do you want to go home and I'll take care of it? Maybe a little ride and drive?"

Draven's cock lurched. Taylor's ride and drives were lusty, loud affairs that consisted of Taylor pounding into him from behind while operating Draven's cock like a gear stick.

He nodded. "I'm not going to refuse an offer like that. God, it drives me crazy just thinking about it."

"Then let's get out of here," Taylor said decisively. "I think we've tainted this office enough with my spunk. Time to taint your bedroom with yours." He turned to leave and Draven grasped him by the arm.

"Tay? I have an appointment next week to see Doctor Frederick. To talk about Jude's wishes. Will you be there with me?" He'd never known his voice could sound so needy. "I know I need to let him go, if that's what he wants. I've thought about it and I guess it's time."

Taylor's face softened. "Of course I'll be there." He took Draven's hand and clasped it tightly. "I'd never let you do anything like that on your own. We'll talk to the doctors and then take it from there."

He pulled Draven to him, warm arms circling his body protectively. Draven fell into the embrace like a drowning man clutching at a life raft. He heard the beat of Taylor's heart in his ear, smelt the warm, living essence of him and heard the love in his voice. This was where he belonged, his future, and it was time to set the past free.

Chapter 12

Taylor sat beside Draven in the quiet hospital room, surrounded by
silence. It was strange; he felt Jude's presence but the young man
hadn't attempted to make any form of contact with him. Last time
the energy Taylor had felt and tapped into had been overwhelming.
Now there was only a sweet serenity and an air of watchfulness. It
was as if Jude knew what was about to happen and was waiting with
bated breath to see how it all turned out.

Draven had been worried for Taylor when they'd first entered
the room, thinking he was going to pass out again. When nothing
had happened, he'd looked relieved but still, his lover's white face
and the grim set to his lips made Taylor's heart ache.

Draven was mute and still, unseeing eyes observing his little
brother with an air of both despair and fear. Taylor held tight to his
cold hand, rubbing his own warm fingers across Draven's skin,
hoping to instil some comfort into what was going to be the most
difficult decision Draven had ever faced.

"That nice doctor said he'd give you as much time as you
needed," Taylor said softly as he stroked the back of Draven's hand.
"He seems like a good enough guy. And that nurse is really lovely.
She has a real sweet spot for Jude, from the looks of it. Has she
looked after him since he got here?"

Draven nodded absently, eyes still focused on the still form
before them.

"Yes. Ally's been a rock, for both of us. I think that woman has
seen me cry more than anyone else ever has." He bit his bottom lip
nervously, gnawing on it until the skin tore and a small drop of blood
blossomed on his pale lips.

Taylor's heart stuttered and his throat tightened. Just for Draven
to admit those moments of weakness was an indication of the stress
he was under. The man was vulnerable, hurting and Taylor just
wanted to fix everything. Yet all he could do was be there for him.
He reached over and took a tissue out of the box on the bedside table.
He handed it to Draven, who patted his bleeding lip, then looked at
the stain with an air of bewilderment.

Draven cleared his throat and looked at Taylor. "So, you seem
okay this time. No passing out and me having to watch you come

around like a chump." He swallowed, and his fingers fidgeted in Taylor's hands.

"Can you, you know, feel him at all?" His other hand reached out and smoothed limp hair from Jude's cheeks, and his face shadowed. He blinked furiously.

Taylor's own helplessness made itself felt in the sudden prickling in his eyes. He sniffed and tried to keep the tears at bay, much as Draven was doing. "I know he's around, but I don't feel him strongly. He feels...settled. Peaceful."

"Do you think he knows?" Draven's choked voice was barely audible. His eyes closed and when he opened them Taylor saw the wetness and the grief reflected in them. Draven was trembling, and Taylor grasped his hand tighter.

"I think he does. I think he knows that his big brother is about to help him go to somewhere he wants to be. With his family—and Pudsey." Taylor lost his voice for a minute as he held back the tears. He took a deep breath.

"You're doing the right thing, baby. I promise."

"It doesn't feel like it," Draven whispered, his tone agonised. "It feels like I'm abandoning him. I have this fucking hole in my heart that he fills and I don't know how I'm going to close it up, Tay. It just isn't right." His voice rose. "I don't think I can do this."

He stood up suddenly, leaving Taylor startled. "I definitely can't do this. Go out there and tell Frederick I've changed my mind." Relief flitted across his face as he stared at Taylor. "This isn't going to happen."

Taylor's stomach lurched as he stood up to intercept his boyfriend. "Dray," he began, and then felt his head swim. He watched through hazy eyes as Draven grew fainter and blurrier and his last conscious image was of Draven's panicked face and arms coming toward him. Then there was only blue.

"Hello, Taylor," Jude said as he stood outlined against the backdrop of what looked like cerulean skies. "It looks like my brother is having a crisis of faith." His gentle smile was affectionate. "This is really tough for him." His voice wavered. "I love him so much and seeing him going through this? It's killing me." He gave a slight watery sniff and a thin chuckle.

"You're all I have to convince him. I'm sorry I'm putting you through this and making contact again. I have no choice."

"I know." Taylor moved toward the younger man. "But it's the toughest thing he's ever had to do."

Jude nodded. "I know. And I wish I could see him for myself, see him, tell him face to face. But this," he waved a hand around him, "this doesn't work that way. It's a miracle I can communicate with you and one I'm really thankful for. Who knew my brother would fall in love with a psychic? It was obviously meant to be."

"What do you want me to tell him?" Taylor leaned forward and touched Jude's cheek. It was warm, vibrant and a world apart from the emaciated figure in the bed in the hospital ward. "What can I tell him to make it better for him?"

Jude shook his head sadly. "There's no easy way to do this. All I can give you is my assurance that this is what I want and need and that one day, I'll see him again. I can't give you a magic talisman or a message from Mum and Dad to convince him I'm real to you because I can't see them yet. All I have is my words, for you to deliver back to him."

Taylor gave a shuddering sigh. "I can only try." He grimaced. "I don't want to stay here with you too long, because he's stressed out enough as it is. This won't be helping him. I need to go back to him."

Jude nodded and reached out a slim hand to caress Taylor's hair. "Tell him you saw me, that this is still what I want and that I love him. He's been so good looking after me, and trying to keep me, but he has to let me go." His eyes flooded with tears.

"He has you now, Taylor, to help him through. He needs the living in his life, not the dead. Tell him he needs to finish that model aeroplane he was building that's still in his cupboard. He was building it for me and when this happened, he stopped. Tell him to go that rock concert of Maroon 5 he always wanted to take me to." Jude sniggered. "He has a real thing for Adam Levine and all his tattoos. I'm sure he used to lick the music magazines I found in his room, the ones that had Adam on the cover. The pages were always slightly buckled and used."

Taylor's eyes widened. "My man has good taste. Adam Levine is damn hot."

The two men grinned at each other and then Jude's face grew serious. "Tell him to do all the things he wanted to do with me, with you. Don't let this destroy him. Please."

Taylor nodded. "I'll do my best." He hesitated, and reached out to touch Jude's arm. "You'll be okay then? I don't even profess to know how this all works, or what it means. My mind is too overwhelmed with everything. But for Draven's sake I need to know myself you're going to be okay when he does what he has to do."

Jude smiled at him. "I'll be fine, honestly."

And Taylor believed him. He didn't know how, or why, but he knew that Jude was telling the truth.

This whole speaking-with-the-almost-dead thing had really thrown him for a loop. His brain hurt and all he wanted to do was get back to Draven. Although the thought of convincing him to switch Jude off made his insides quail, he knew deep inside that it was the right choice for Draven to make.

Jude reached over and laid warm lips on Taylor's forehead. "I'm glad he's got you." His voice choked up. "Take care of my big brother, Taylor. See you on the other side one day." His voice grew fainter and his figure blurred and shimmered and when Taylor blinked his eyes, he was staring up once again into anxious, red-rimmed, silver-grey eyes. The man behind them was pale, his mouth tight, but his face softened as Taylor stared at him from the chair in the corner where Draven had obviously placed him.

"Tay, you there?" Draven's voice was choked. "Christ, I'm getting fucking sick of this. I never know whether you're going to come back to me."

Taylor tried to blink the fuzziness from his eyes and sat up gingerly. "I'll always come back to you," he murmured. "Right now, I'd love some water. I feel like puking." He retched and Draven hurriedly picked up a glass from the side table and went over to the small corner basin to fill it up. He came back and presented it to Taylor.

"Thanks." Taylor took deep gulps and the dizziness and disorientation he'd felt on coming back into the real world lessened.

Draven perched beside him on the chair arm and stroked stray curls of hair back behind his ears. "Will I ever get used to that?" he asked quietly. "Seeing you drift off somewhere else? Thank God I was there to catch you again or else you'd have found yourself on the floor. Can't you do this sort of thing when you're sitting down, or sleeping?" Draven was trying to be cheery but the sorrow in his eyes belied his attempt.

Taylor gave a soft chuckle. "I wish I could tell you I could. I guess we'll just have to make sure you'll always be around, won't we?"

They looked at each other steadfastly and then Draven sighed. It was a deep, heart-wrenching sigh and Taylor wished he could lift the burden of Draven's decision from him and throw it into a deep, dark hole.

"You saw him." It wasn't a question.

Taylor nodded. "Yes. And he says switching the machinery is the right decision for him. He's tired. He wants to go home, wherever that is." He snorted, weary. "I'm not even going to go down the route again of trying to figure out where it is when I go. For all I know it could be a huge white hotel in the middle of somewhere with room service, good wine, a hot tub and a naked man with a six pack and a huge dick servicing my every desire."

Draven raised an eyebrow, a slight grin on his face. "*That's* your idea of heaven?"

Taylor shrugged. "Absolutely. I can live with that."

The sheer absurdity of his statement had both men staring at each other then bursting into a fit of chuckles. Taylor was glad he'd been able to lift Draven's spirits just a little. When the chuckles subsided, Taylor stood up and went over to hug Draven, holding him tightly.

"I didn't know you built model aeroplanes," he murmured into Draven's ear. Draven stiffened and Taylor carried on, his voice teasing. "I also didn't know you had a crush on the very sexy Adam Levine. We share that, by the way."

Draven turned and it was as if a light was finally going on his head. His eyes shone with tears and his face, while still etched with grief, was full of wonder. "He really was with you, wasn't he?"

Taylor frowned as Draven rushed ahead. "I mean I know you said he was, and I believed you, but hearing you say those things…it just makes it more real, you know? I never doubted you, Tay; I just needed to really understand that this was what he wanted…"

Taylor's lips stopped Draven's words midway as he kissed him, and they breathed into each other's mouths as tongues and lips came together. Taylor's hands slid around Draven's waist as he pressed closer. The kiss was long, deep, and in it, Taylor tried to convey every iota of feeling and love he had for the man in his arms. When it was over, they stood clinched together as if they were the last two people standing on a shattered earth.

"It's time, isn't it?" Draven said finally, his voice muffled against Taylor's ear, buried in his curls.

"Yes, baby. I think so." Taylor moved away and tugged Draven toward the bed. "Sit down. Talk to your brother; tell him everything you want to get out of your soul. I'll go find Doctor Frederick and tell him you're ready." He pushed Draven into the chair at the side of the bed and placed a soft kiss on the top of his head and then disappeared out of the door.

*****

Draven sat still in the chair, taking deep breaths as he readied himself for what was to come. He wasn't ready. He was nowhere near fucking ready for this momentous decision but he knew deep inside that it was the right thing to do.

"I hope you can hear me, little brother," he murmured softly. "I'm glad you and Taylor got a chance to meet. He's an incredible individual and I know, little brother, that I am properly in love for the first time in my life. He means the world to me." He chuckled as he stroked Jude's pale hand. "The man might get ideas above his station and he's already an arrogant little shit. Him knowing I'm that much crazy about him would just give him carte blanche to make my life a constant fest of smug 'I know you love me' crap."

His voice faltered. "He tells me this is what you need and I trust him, more than anyone I've ever known. And you obviously trust him too to tell him about my Adam Levine crush. I'd kick your arse if you were here now for letting that cat out of the bag."

His eyes were hot with tears and he let them roll down his cheeks. "I love you, little brother. I tried to do right by you, and maybe I was selfish keeping you around, but not having you around like you used to be these last few years broke my heart. Maybe we were both just waiting for Taylor to come along so I get this chance to do this. I need him, Jude. I thank God every day I wake to him for coming into my life."

There was a noise at the door and Draven turned to see Taylor standing there, eyes awash with tears and a look on his face that promised the world to Draven. Doctor Frederick stood beside Taylor, face wreathed in sympathy, Sister Alison behind him. Her round face was warm and a welcome sight to Draven.

Doctor Frederick moved into the room and regarded Draven compassionately. "Taylor says you're ready for the machine to be switched off, Draven. I'm sorry to have to ask this at a time like this but there's a form I need you to sign before I can do that." He shrugged apologetically. "The perils of a bureaucracy and a 'cover the hospital's arse' mentality, I'm afraid."

Draven couldn't find any words so he nodded mutely. Taylor moved over to him and his dark brown eyes regarded him lovingly. "I'm here, love. Right beside you. If you're sure..." his voice trailed off. Alison bustled past the doctor into the room and clasped Draven's hands in hers.

"Baby, you are so damn brave. I don't know what made you decide you were ready, maybe it was this gorgeous man standing next to you, but it's the right decision. I've never wanted to push you into it; it's something you've had to figure out for yourself." She handed him a worn clipboard and Draven didn't even read it. He simply looked for the place he was supposed to sign and through eyes blurred with tears, he scribbled his signature and handed the board back to Alison. He though he saw the shine of tears in her eyes as he did so.

Alison laid the clipboard down and enveloped him into a hug that was warm and maternal. Her hands stroked his back as he burrowed into her massive bosom, his tears soaking her uniform as she consoled him with soft sounds of comfort.

He smelt Taylor before he felt him, his warm, spicy masculine scent like home as he stepped behind Draven and wrapped his long arms around his back. Draven luxuriated in being sandwiched between his lover and a woman who had comforted him more times than he could count over the years.

Doctor Frederick cleared his throat as he fiddled at the tubes and lines coming out of Jude's frail body. "Draven, do you want to say anything else before I do this?"

Draven sniffed and nodded, extricating himself from the octopus tentacles of the people who held him. "Yes." He moved over to Jude and brushed the limp hair off his forehead.

"Goodbye, buddy. I love you so damn much. I hope when you see Mum and Dad you tell them I love them too and one day I hope to see you all again." He felt the closing of his throat and the bittersweet wrench in his chest.

"I'll take Taylor to see Maroon 5 and I promise you I'll finish building that aeroplane and fly it for you when it's done. Rest in peace, Jude. I love you."

By now he was a wreck, body shuddering and jerking with sobs and Taylor reached out and drew him in, his voice thick when he spoke.

"God, babe, come here. I've got you."

Draven collapsed into protective arms, and a broad chest that promised familiarity and strength. The two of them clung to each other and Draven vaguely heard Alison crooning something to Jude over the bed and the doctor's quiet voice as he asked to help him.

Draven didn't want to—God, he really didn't want to see his brother slip away, watch as the machines keeping Jude alive were switched off and he simply stopped existing at all. Yet he knew he *had* to or he would never forgive himself. He burrowed into Taylor like a mole and let Taylor's strong arms and whispered comforts strengthen him. Watching Doctor Fredrick switch off the machines, Draven reached for thoughts of he and Jude catching frogs, swimming in the river and hunting tadpoles; sweet memories of the awed look on his twelve-year-old brother's face when he said a girl had kissed him for the first time.

It seemed like forever but was only a few minutes. The sounds of the life-giving support gradually ceased, and with it the rise and fall of Jude's chest. Draven's eyes were strangely dry and as Taylor's arms tightened around him, he wondered bemusedly when it would all hit him. When the world would stop turning and the grief in his chest would stop hurting. Behind him he heard sniffles and the loud blowing of a nose. Alison was feeling Jude's departure as strongly as he was from the sounds of it.

Fredrick looked at Draven with sad eyes. "It's over," he said simply. "He didn't suffer. I thought you might like to be with him. Alison will have someone come in soon to take care of him. I'm sorry for your loss, Mr. Samuels." He pressed Draven's arm tightly and left the room.

Draven managed to pull himself from Taylor and walked unsteadily to the bed. Jude looked no different than before; he was still pale and frail. Draven liked to think he saw the beginnings of a slight smile on his face but he thought that might simply be wishful thinking.

"He's been gone a long time, Draven," Alison said, her tone soft. "Now he's gone home, where he belongs."

Draven nodded and placed a kiss on Jude's cool forehead. "She'll take good care of you, little one," he whispered. "I have to go now. But one day I know we'll see each other again."

For a while he and Taylor sat there with Jude as Draven held his hand and came to terms with the fact his brother was truly gone. The doctor came in about an hour later and said gently they needed to move Jude and Draven winced but nodded. Taylor held his hand, squeezing it gently as they stood up.

He kissed Jude again then turned to the hovering form of Taylor waiting anxiously behind him. "I guess there's nothing else I can do here. Take me home, Tay. I just want to go to bed and cuddle up with you and not think about anything else." The numb feeling in his chest lessened a bit at Taylor's warm smile and concern.

"I can do that. Come on then, let's get you home. Maybe we need to use an old friend's remedy for feeling stressed or down. Chamomile tea. Leslie swears by it."

Draven grimaced. "Not so sure I like that idea. A stiff whiskey sounds like a better bet."

He gave one last lingering look at the young boy in the bed behind him.

Alison reached out and hugged him. "You look after yourself, Draven honey. I know you won't be around much anymore but don't be a stranger. Pop in and see me now and then and let me know how you're doing."

Draven kissed her plump cheek tenderly. "I promise I will. You don't get rid of me that easy." He swallowed. "Alison, you won't let anyone touch him, or anything, will you? I need to arrange the funeral, it will be a cremation, but I don't want him getting cut or anything like that."

Alison laid a large finger on his mouth. "Hush, young man. I promise you nothing is going to happen to that sweet boy. I will take real good care of him for you until you're ready to take him away from here." She looked at Taylor. "You make sure you look after this man, you hear? He's very special to all of us."

"He's very special to me too, Alison," Taylor murmured. "I promise I'll take care of him."

She narrowed her eyes at him. "You are special too. I can sense it. I know you have the gift. My ancestors had the same thing. It passed me by but I still recognise it when I see it. If that helped these two sort things out, then I'm really grateful to you. And if you ever see that young scamp again," she waved at the still figure in the bed, "you make sure and tell him Nurse Ally misses him but she's glad he's at peace."

Taylor's eyes welled up and Draven reached over and slid his finger under a tear that threatened to drop.

"I will," Taylor said. "I doubt I'll see him again but if I do, I will." He sniffed and wiped his sleeve under his nose.

She nodded in satisfaction. "Then get off home, the two of you and get some rest. Draven, you take care of this young man. He's a keeper."

Draven glanced at Taylor, who held his gaze. That look seemed to say everything Draven was feeling and he was warmed knowing that Taylor seemed to feel the same way about him.

Taylor leaned in and whispered in his ear. "I heard what you said to Jude. I really liked it all, apart from that bit about being an arrogant little shit." He pouted.

Despite the feeling of grief in his heart, Draven couldn't stop a soft laugh at the adorable man before him and he pressed a swift kiss to his lips. "I meant every word of it. But we can talk about this later. Come on, let's get out of here."

He pulled Taylor by the hand and together, they left Jude's room and the hospital behind.

Chapter 13

Taylor kept his hand on Draven's leg the whole drive home. Draven was pale and quiet, and while Taylor wanted to simply take him in his arms and never let go, he knew his lover needed time. Time to process that he would no longer make the journey home from the hospital again. Time to realise he would no longer see his brother each week, or read stories to him. Draven needed space to properly grieve now that the thin and fragile thread biding the brothers together had been severed.

Since they'd left the silent hospital ward where Jude lay, Draven hadn't said a word. He'd walked with Taylor to the car, gotten in, adjusted his seatbelt and started the car. He'd looked calm but Taylor sensed the churning roils of emotion beneath the façade. He'd not been disposed to talk himself much anyway, given what had just happened. He hadn't known Jude long but even in such a short time, he felt a sense of loss and regret. He could only imagine how Draven felt.

Taylor stared out of the window, watching the scenery and London buildings flash by.

Draven cleared his throat now and then and Taylor saw the bob of his Adam's apple as he swallowed, his hands clenching sporadically at the wheel. Taylor simply tightened his grip on Draven's leg, letting him know he was there for him.

Finally, as they neared home and Draven pulled into park, he spoke. His voice was tight, barely controlled. "Thanks for being there with me."

Taylor nodded. "Of course. Where else would I be?" He squeezed Draven's leg gently.

The car stopped and they got out and made their way up the few stairs to Draven's front door. As they went inside, it was as if all of Draven's control went. His shoulders shuddered and he gasped, deep, wrenching breaths of sheer grief, as tears streamed down his face, and he reached out blindly for Taylor. He gathered Draven to him, wrapping arms around that tried to comfort and console, as tears of his own trickled down his cheeks at his lover's distress.

"If it was the right thing to do, why do I feel so damn empty?" Draven's face, wet with tears, was pressed against Taylor's shoulder. Taylor hugged him close, wondering what to say.

"You spent the best part of three years looking after him," he murmured softly even as his heart ached at Draven's pain. "You were his big brother, and you loved him. I could tell that he adored you too. This was the hardest part for him as well, knowing you would be upset but still keeping his wish."

Draven's voice was muffled by Taylor's shirt when he spoke again. "I couldn't have done this without you by my side, you know that, right? You..." he swallowed and looked up at Taylor, his eyes red rimmed and swollen—still he was the most beautiful man Taylor had ever seen. "You make things better, in every way. I don't tell you that enough." His hand came up to caress Taylor's cheek and he felt warmth in his chest at the look in Draven's eyes. For a moment he was breathless. No man had ever looked at him like that before. He didn't want to jinx the moment by reading more into it that was warranted so he smiled instead and placed a gentle kiss on Draven's cool lips, moving away swiftly lest he make a fool of himself.

"Thank you. I feel the same way about you." He released his grip on Draven. "Are you hungry, babe? I can make us pasta if you like, if you don't mind me rummaging in your kitchen for scraps to use. I know you don't tend to have much in there, so I guess I need to be careful when I open the damn fridge that something doesn't grab me and try and pull me in, a rogue bit of mould that's gone mutant." He was aware he was rambling but he was still overwhelmed at the look he'd seen in Draven's eyes and the way he himself felt about the man standing in front of him with a quizzical expression on his face.

He wanted to say the words "I love you" so badly, let out the feelings that dwelt deep in his heart. But he felt raw, as if by saying them right at this minute among Draven's pain that it would cheapen them. Instead, Taylor ignored the impulse and reached down to take out a saucepan from the kitchen cupboard under the sink. "I suppose I'll have to get creative; maybe I can find a new use for out-of-date yoghurt and slightly green potatoes..."

"Taylor." Draven smiled and leaned over to place a finger on his lips. Taylor stopped midway between the action of placing the saucepan on the stove top and turning on the burner.

Draven took it from him and placed it on the top of the kitchen island. Then he reached out, tugged at Taylor's hips and drew him into his body, pressing Taylor back against the island and taking his willing mouth in a punishing yet completely earth-shattering kiss that made his toes tingle and his balls ache. His arse clenched in delight as Draven's hands moved behind him and grasped it tightly as he ground his groin against him. His mouth was being assaulted by a tongue that knew no boundaries and lips that bruised his with the intensity of the kiss. Food forgotten, they clutched each other eagerly, soft sighs of pleasure and moans of content echoing through the still kitchen.

Finally Draven let him go, and Taylor blinked, disoriented at the loss of his lover's mouth.

"What spooked you?" Draven whispered. "What did you see in my face or eyes that made you all flustered?"

Taylor flushed at the fact he'd been so transparent. "Nothing, I just wanted to do something nice for you…" his voice trailed away at Draven's raised eyebrow, something which made the man even sexier than usual. The sight of that eyebrow above slate-grey eyes caused Taylor's pulse to quicken and his mouth to dry.

"Tay, tell me." Draven brushed his lips across Taylor's throat and he moaned, the sound embarrassing him with its sense of need.

"I, I…you just drive me damn crazy and I love you. But this isn't the time to tell you, you just came back from the hospital after losing your brother again and I don't want to confuse you or say something to upset you…"

He groaned as warm lips found the pulse in his throat and kissed it gently, like the slow tickle of a butterfly as its fluttered its satin wings against skin. The longing he had to be both possessed by Draven and possess him in turn, mind, body and soul, was bubbling below heated skin and he feared he might explode if he didn't let it loose.

"I can see it in your eyes," Draven murmured, "just as you can see it in mine. Shall I go first? Tell you how I feel about you? How you've taken my heart and made it feel something I've never had before? How the sight of your body makes me hard, makes me want to rip your clothes off and take you?"

Taylor was rock hard in his jeans now as he closed his eyes and gave into the sensations Draven was causing as he pressed close to his body. "Shall I tell you that you're the only man I ever want to wake up to, to kiss, to make love to?" Draven's voice deepened. "I *know* what just happened, and what I lost. I also know what I gained. A beautiful, funny, sexy, infuriating, incredible human being with a talent only the gods could give. You are something very special indeed, Taylor Abelard. And *that's* why I love you."

The words "I love you" were there, in the kitchen, in Taylor's ears, cemented in his heart and the world stopped. With trembling fingers, he traced the contours of Draven's face, marvelling at the joy filling his soul and warming him from top to bottom.

Draven's eyes darkened and he captured Taylor's lips in yet another rough and passionate kiss. Taylor surrendered absolutely, closing his eyes and rejoicing in the simple fact that Draven loved him. And damn the rest of world and its tragedies, its harsh reality and its blurred lines of imaginations and dreams and its ability to intrude in the moments that counted. *This—this* was the moment that Taylor knew deep in his bones and his heart that had been meant to be, a moment where he felt loved, special, and was someone's rock, the person they depended on as much as he did them.

Draven relaxed in his arms, his eager, questing lips on his, and the feel of both his solidity and vulnerability pressed against Taylor's body. In the warmth that followed as contentment and passion flooded Taylor's body, he swore he heard a young man's chuckle as warm fingers brushed his face and said goodbye.

Six months later...

Draven fidgeted as he sat at the intimate, candlelit table in a secluded alcove of Galileo's. His fingers drummed a nervous beat on the table as he watched Taylor make his way back from the bathroom. The small box in his pocket knocked against his hip each time he moved as it made its presence known.

The box and its contents had been foremost in Draven's mind this past week, ever since he'd picked it up from the jeweller. He smiled as Taylor sat down opposite him, dark eyes shining in the candlelight, black hair outlined in the dim light like a halo around Taylor's head. Not for the first time Draven marvelled at the being that was his lover and hopefully, soon to be something else.

"Sorry about that," Taylor grimaced as he leaned over and brushed long, graceful fingers over Draven's tapping fingers. "I think that beer went right through me. I'm peeing like a bloody racehorse at a competition."

Draven shook his head in amusement. "Thanks for that image. I plan this whole romantic dinner and all I can think of now is a bloody horse peeing in a bloody bucket."

Taylor chuckled. "I don't know how they actually do it, it's just one of those sayings you hear." He gazed around the restaurant. "Have you seen the dessert menu yet? I really fancy that chocolate thingy they had on the Specials board when we came in. Eddie's really proud of that one; I think it's called 'Sublime Chocolate Overdose' or something like that…" His voice tailed off as Draven reached over and placed a finger on his lips, effectively stopping him mid flow. Taylor's eyes widened.

Draven smiled at him. "I have something I need to say to you, and I need to do it now before I lose my nerve." He removed his finger and reached into his pocket.

Taylor blinked in confusion. "Uhmm, yeah sure. What is it?" His face grew worried. "Everything is okay, isn't it? This isn't an 'I'm breaking up with you' occasion, is it? Because I am *so* not ready for that conversation…just so you know. I mean, I've just moved in."

Taylor had indeed moved in with Draven, giving up the house he shared with Leslie. Despite his nervousness at what he was about to do, the panicked look on Taylor's face made Draven grin. "No, babe, definitely not that."

His heart was racing now, his throat dry and his stomach in knots. He stood up then knelt down at Taylor's side. He'd debated with himself how he wanted this to go down and had decided on doing it the old-fashioned way. The expression on Taylor's face was a mix of surprise, hope and panic.

The noise in the restaurant seemed to diminish in Draven's ears as he took a deep breath and threw caution to the wind. He'd practiced this speech in the mirror so many times and yet—now he was here, before Taylor, and his well-rehearsed words were forgotten.

"Taylor, I hope you don't think this is too soon, but I think we've been through quite a lot together, and I know how *I* feel, and know how *you* feel, we say it enough to each other." Taylor gazed at him with eyes that seemed to drink him in. His lips parted and

Draven wanted to kiss them and tell him that way what he was trying to ask. He cleared his throat.

"There's no other man I want to share my life with, and fuck, this sounds so damn mushy and sentimental, but I don't know how else to say it." He took a deep breath, seeing the bright, sudden, sheen in Taylor's brown eyes and the slight flaring of his nostrils. "I love you, and I want it to be real." He tripped over himself to amend that last comment. "I mean, it's real, of course it is, but I want it to be even more than that. Taylor Abelard," he brought out the small box that his nerveless fingers had been clenched around in his pocket, "Will you do me the honour of marrying me? Being my husband one day when you're ready?" Taylor's quick, indrawn breath made Draven's stomach clench in fear. "I mean, only if you're ready, I don't want to rush into this if you don't feel it's the right time..."

This time, it was his mouth that was stopped by long, warm fingers as Taylor pushed his chair back and with his other hand, drew Draven up off his knees. Draven stood, slightly unsure of what the answer was going to be.

He got it soon enough as Taylor pulled him into a kiss that curled his toes, made his cock reach for the heavens and sent a tingle through his body, right into his very marrow.

Lips that tasted faintly of citrus and rocket from the salad Taylor had eaten, lips that were so sweet and welcoming that they drew Draven into them like a moth intent on suicide by flying into light and heat. Taylor had finally stopped smoking completely and his mouth was all the sweeter for it. The world stopped as Draven's eyes closed and all he could feel was Taylor's warmth and love flooding his soul. Finally he was released and vaguely heard a clapping sound in the distance as his senses returned to normal.

Taylor pressed his forehead against Draven's and exhaled a sweet breath against his skin. "God, you know how to make a man feel special. That was like something out of a rom-com. And yes, my beautiful lover, I would love to be your husband. Nothing could make me happier."

The restaurant patrons were on their feet, clapping and smiling at the spectacle unfolding before them. Taylor watched with hooded eyes as Draven's unsteady fingers opened the box and took out the palladium ring he'd had specially designed. It was a simple band of smooth metal, with two diamonds embedded into the middle.

Draven gently slid it onto Taylor's finger. He felt a sense of satisfaction. It fit perfectly. He took out its twin and slid it onto his own finger then lifted his eyes to gaze at Taylor.

"Now it's official." Out of the corner of his eye, Gideon and Eddie standing together, watching. They came over and hugged them, Gideon clapping Draven on his back as he grinned widely.

"Bloody well done, Draven. That took some guts, my friend." He slid a sly sideways glance at Eddie. "Maybe you've started a trend…who knows?"

Eddie's fair face flushed with pleasure as he reached out and pulled Taylor into a bear hug. "Yeah, you never know…Taylor, congratulations, mate. So pleased for you both."

Draven flinched as long, muscled freckled arms headed his way and was pleasantly surprised when Eddie pulled him for a hug too. "You make him so damn happy," Eddie whispered in Draven's ear. "I guess my original impression of you wasn't all that accurate. That makes me really glad."

Gideon waved over a passing waiter as the restaurant got back to normal and guests sat back down with friendly glances their way and the occasional "Well done to you" nod.

"Brent, bring us a bottle of the good champers for these guys. I think they've earned it, don't you?"

Brent nodded, his shaggy head of blond hair falling around his face as he grinned. "I think so, boss. Be right back." He sidled past the tables as he made his way to the bar.

Gideon raised a knowing eyebrow at Eddie. "I think we've outstayed our welcome," he smirked. "Let's let the lovebirds be alone."

Eddie grinned, his freckled face warm with affection. "Congrats again, guys. It couldn't happen to a nicer couple." He cast a scorching glance at Gideon who gave a heated look of his own back. Draven wondered whether there might be another wedding on the cards soon.

Eddie saw his look and smiled widely. "Now we just have to find Leslie a mate and the three of us will all be paired off." He patted Taylor on the arm then disappeared with a smiling Gideon.

Draven saw the fleeting look of guilt cross Taylor's face. It had worried his fiancé—how right it felt being able to call Taylor that—

that Leslie had been left alone now that both Eddie and Taylor were gone to pastures new.

To put Taylor's worries to rest, Draven had made sure he did everything he could with his and Clay's connections to get Leslie an affordable studio flat in Kennington, not far from where the house was. Thanks to a generous boss, who seemed to adore the ground Leslie walked on, he had even got an increase in salary to help him settle in on his own. He reached out a hand and caressed Taylor's cheek.

"Tay, babe, Leslie will be fine. He's a spitfire of a soul and if anyone can look after himself, that man can. And just think how excited he's going to be when he hears he has a wedding to fit us out for. The man is going to wet himself."

Taylor nodded and looked back at him with more love than Draven knew what to do with. He wanted nothing more than to take him home, throw him onto the bed and make love to him until he forgot his own name.

He wanted to taste Taylor, feel his skin against his own and marvel at the man who'd just agreed to be his husband. Instead, he sat down and motioned to Taylor to do the same, and watched as Brent poured glasses of champagne for them then disappeared like a wraith, leaving them in peace.

Taylor raised his glass. "To my fiancé. Good health, good loving and great sex. And may there continue to be lots of that." He chuckled.

Draven inclined his head and raised his glass, to clink it against Taylor's. "To my sexy fiancé, definitely to the good sex and even more loving." They drank deeply then toasts done, they set their glasses down on the table.

Taylor quirked an eyebrow at Draven.

"I don't know about you, but I'm as horny as fuck and I really want to get you home to bed. What say we drink this champagne very quickly then get home?"

Draven couldn't agree more with that plan. He reached over and took the bottle and topped up their glasses. "I love a man who knows what he wants. Home it is."

The smouldering look Taylor gave him made Draven begrudge even the time it took to finish the bottle until the two of them were giggling like school boys and touching each other at a pace that was about to get them kicked out for public lewdness.

Later, as Draven watched the lean, muscled form of his lover ride him as if there was no tomorrow, his skin shining with sweat and that wicked mouth devouring his, he took time to close his eyes and simply bask in the joy that suffused his heart at having such a man in his life.

As Taylor leaned down to whisper words of love in his ear, kissing Draven's heated flesh, Draven knew that somewhere, not too far away, Jude was happy for him. His heart still ached at what he'd lost but was overfilled with love at what he'd found.

With Taylor in his life, he'd come full circle from being alone to being complete and he had the feeling that life would never be quite the same again.

The End

AUTHOR'S NOTE

There is an element of my own experience in this story with Jude, as there are in all of my stories. I think one of the wonderful things about writing for me is the ability to take personal events and write them into a fictional account of someone else. There's a sort of solace in doing so. You'll also find a lot of my own beliefs and opinions squirreled away in my stories. So, not only have I been to the places my characters live and work in; I also try to impart some of the things I believe and learned along the way.

ABOUT THE AUTHOR

Susan Mac Nicol is a self-confessed bookaholic, an avid watcher of videos of sexy pole-dancing men, a self-confessed geek and nerd, and in love with her Smartphone. This little treasure is called 'the boyfriend' by her longsuffering husband, who says if it vibrated there'd be no need for him. Susan hasn't had the heart to tell him there's an app for that.

A lover of walks in the forest, theatre productions, dabbling her toes in the cold North Sea and the vibrant city of London where you can experience all four seasons in a day, she is a hater of pantomime (please don't tar and feather her), duplicitous people, bigotry and self-righteous idiots. She likes to think of herself as a 'half full' kind of gal, although sometimes that philosophy is sorely tested.

In an ideal world, Susan Mac Nicol would be Queen of England and banish all the bad people to the Never Never Lands of Wherever-Who Cares. As that's not going to happen, she contents herself with writing her HEA stories and pretending that, just for a little while, good things happen to good people.

OTHER BOOKS BY SUSAN MAC NICOL

Stripped Bare
Saving Alexander
Worth Keeping
Double Alchemy
Double Alchemy: Climax
Love and Punishment

THE MEN OF LONDON SERIES

Love You Senseless

THE STARLIGHT SERIES

Cassandra by Starlight
Together in Starlight

Did you enjoy this book? Drop us a line and say so! We love to hear from readers, and so do our authors. To connect, visit www.boroughspublishinggroup.com online, send comments directly to info@boroughspublishinggroup.com, or friend us on Facebook and Twitter. And be sure to check back regularly for contests and new releases in your favorite subgenres of romance!

Are you an aspiring writer? Check out www.boroughspublishinggroup.com/submit and see if we can help you make your dreams come true.